THE STELLAR LEGION

THE STELLAR LEGION

LEGION

E. C. TUBB

WILDSIDE PRESS

INTRODUCTION

BY PHILIP HARBOTTLE

The Stellar Legion was first published in the UK by Scion Ltd in 1954, and was one of Tubb's best early novels. Notwithstanding, because of the unfair stigma applied to all science fiction novels issued by the minor British 'mushroom' publishers in the postwar decade, it remained out of print for some 45 years, before I was able to arrange for its reprinting by a US small press.

That the novel was overlooked for so long was particularly unfortunate because its militaristic background had anticipated many of the themes of Robert A. Heinlein's widely known and acclaimed novel *Starship Troopers*, to which it was a fascinating precursor.

Heinlein's book appeared in the USA five years *after* Tubb's novel, and caused a storm of controversy, both pro and con. In England, British author Tubb would have a good reason to shake his head and smile wryly. Whilst his book was long out of print and almost forgotten, Heinlein's novel went on to win the coveted Hugo Award for 1959.

Starship Troopers centred on the theme of the justification for a strong military force; in Heinlein's novel, his soldiers save the human race by fighting against inimical aliens, the 'Bugs'. Heinlein's most assiduous critic, Alexei Panshin, referred to the book as 'a militaristic polemic' that shows 'military life in the most glamorous terms possible', giving 'a direct philosophical justification for government veterans, and militarism as a way of life'.

E.C. Tubb was always a largely inspirational writer. That is to say, he was not someone who cold-bloodedly worked out his plot before he began writing. He required only to work out his basic opening setting and characters, and then inspiration took over, fuelled by Tubb's especial forte: logic! Once he had created a basic situation, Tubb was able to extrapolate—*logically*—that such and such a situation was likely to occur, and then his novel took shape. The trick was to find that initial inspiration!

In 1999 Tubb told me that the initial spark of inspiration for *The Stellar Legion* came from his own reading of L. Ron Hubbard's novel *Final Blackout* (1940,1948). Hubbard's novel is well known, and has been either critically acclaimed as a militaristic masterpiece, or condemned as a fascist tract. It tells of how an army officer known as 'The Lieutenant' survives a devastating world war and its aftermath, to become the Dictator of England. What sparked Tubb's imagination, he told me, was the idea of an individual who is born and raised in the midst of war, his whole being shaped by pain and terror. Assuming that such an individual could survive, how would he do it, and what would he become?

From this plot germ, Tubb developed the story of an orphan, Mike Wilson, whose early boyhood is spent in forced labour on Earth. Having been adjudged a murderer at the age of 17, he is sentenced to be deported across space, to a newly formed penal planet, Stellar. Here, he rises through the ranks of a ruthless military regime to become a sergeant in the Stellar Legion. (Like the noted American writer Wilson Tucker, Tubb was fond of using the real names of friends and acquaintances for his characters. 'Mike Wilson' was a friend and partner of Arthur C. Clarke, and a frequent visitor to the meetings of the London Circle of fans and authors. Trivia buffs might also like to note that 'Mike Wilson' was the name of the hero of Tubb's 1961 strip cartoon war story, *Hellfire Landing*!)

Heinlein's novel closely parallels much of Tubb's story of Wilson in its account of his narrator, Rico, and his gruelling basic military training as a young man, followed by his graduation. But to some commentators, Heinlein's award-winning novel fails to engage on the human level, being little more than a history of the making of a soldier, and a glorification of the military system. Tubb's novel, on the other hand, is much more intriguing and darkly ambivalent. The rigours of Wilson's military training are horrifying, and there is no glorification of war. Tubb's prose—as ever—is lean and unsentimental, and Wilson's actions are driven purely by a relentless logic, an exercise in personal survival.

What makes Tubb's novel even more intriguing is how the story of Wilson becomes subsumed in the wider theme of the threat to peace to mankind (spread over several colonized solar systems and unified under a Federation of Man) posed by a highly trained and powerful military force. Tubb posits a military elite shaped by the motivation of personal survival dependent on obedience. *But what would happen if a soldier from that elite were to be given a contra-survival order—when to obey that command could mean his own death?*

With great panache, Tubb resolves his themes in a logical manner, culminating in a fascinating clash between his two other main characters. Laurance, the Director of the Federation of Man obsessed with the maintenance of a hard-won peace in the aftermath of interstellar war, versus Hogarth, fanatical military commander of the Stellar Legion. Tubb became engrossed with the writing of this novel, and told me that at the time it appeared, he was actually contemplating writing a sequel. In the new novel, Wilson became a lieutenant, and then…? Alas, not long after the novel appeared, its publishers, Scion Ltd., fell victim to the icy wind of change that blew across the UK publishing scene, and the sequel was never written. This is surely a matter of great regret.

In 1964, as a callow youth writing in my own fanzine, *E.C. Tubb—An Evaluation*, I said then of *The Stellar Legion*, that "it is worth noting the similarity between this novel and Heinlein's much later *Starship Troopers*. Tubb wins hands down in every respect, in my opinion."

Having just reread Tubb's novel, I see no reason to change my youthful opinion! But you don't just have to take my word for it—thanks to Wildside, you can now read Tubb's lost classic for yourself!

CHAPTER I

FRUITS OF WARFARE

He was born in the midst of pain and terror, on a planet ripped and torn by war, and the arrogant throb of atomic destruction made a savage accompaniment to his baby wail. His mother never lived to suckle him, she, along with fifty million others died in the unleashed hell of the last missile raid on Earth and his father had vanished, a nameless memory, somewhere in the wastes of outer space.

Before he was a year old his skin had been seared by the agony of radiation burns, his food reduced to a nauseous mess, his comfort far less than that of the infinitely more valuable farm animals. He never knew love or affection, the gentle touch of a mother's hand or the riotous fun of parental play.

He never had a toy, a nurse, a playmate or the understanding of an adult dedicated to his welfare.

They washed him, fed him, dressed his wounds, and then they left him, one of a hundred others, to live or die as nature saw fit. Soon he learned that crying only brought harsh words and rough hands so he ceased from crying and lay, hour after hour, day after day, month after month, staring with bright baby eyes at the low ceiling of the hospital, listening to the sobbing moans of men blasted beyond all semblance of human beings.

That he managed to heal his tormented body was a wonder. That he forced himself to walk, to see, to hang grimly onto his awareness was something never to be understood. That he lived at all was a miracle.

When he was eight they put him to work, toiling among the shattered ruins of cities, helping the broken remains of what had once been men to clear away the debris and build anew. The war had receded from Earth by then, the great ships of space were locked in conflict above the planets of alien suns, and other men and women, other children learned what it was to cringe helpless as atomic missiles drove in from the night of space.

When he was ten most of the independent worlds had fallen and now smarted beneath the rule of Earth, their fleets broken, their soil burned, their proud men and women accepting the inevitable and relinquishing their dream of self-rule. They grumbled, glowered, then, as reason returned and the ghastly price of liberty cried in pain-filled voices around them, swallowed their pride and set to work to build the Federation of Man.

When he was twelve they took him from the cities and set him to work at reclaiming the poisoned soil. He had a name by now, and a number, and of the two the number was the most important.

He worked from dawn to dusk, shovelling the radiation-tainted dirt into great hoppers where it was neutralised, enriched with humus and fertilisers, and replaced ready for the planting. It was hard work, thankless work, and dangerous. The radiations, even though nullified by the passage of time, still retained enough force to inflict ugly burns, and he sweltered in heavy protective clothing as he worked on the edge of the blue-limned desert that had once been Kent.

He had an overseer, a tough, scarred veteran of space, a man embittered by his own incompetence and in perpetual pain from his badly fitted artificial legs. A short, stocky man, addicted to crudely distilled spirits and with a sadistic streak to bely his outer manner. A man, who for some obscure reason, hated the thin, grey-eyed, dark-haired boy with the blue scar of an old wound marring the side of his neck and blotching his cheek.

"Hey, you," he yelled. "Wilson."

"Yes?" Wilson stood, fighting the sudden knotting of his stomach muscles, the thick hood of his protective clothing thrown back from his pale, blue-scarred features. The overseer snarled and walked painfully forward.

"How many times do I have to tell you, you swine? When you speak to me you call me 'sir'. Get it?"

"Yes, sir."

"That's better. Now grab some food and get back to work. We're behind schedule and the inspectors will be coming to examine progress in a week or two. I want to show them that we can do our share."

Wilson hesitated. "I'm due for a rest period, sir."

"Are you arguing with me?" Anger convulsed the overseer's heavy features and his right hand clenched into a club of bone and sinew. "You heard what I said. Eat and get back to work." He glowered at the other nine boys making up the work party.

"That goes for you, too. All of you. I've had my eye on this group, idling and wasting time when you thought that no one could see you. Well, now you're going to pay for it, and you'll work double shifts until I tell you to stop."

Silence fell over the little group and one of the boys, a delicate-faced youngster with a twisted leg and a hunched back, began to cry. The sound seemed to touch off a devil in the stocky man's heart and he swung, his muddy eyes glinting as he stared at the clustered youths.

"Who's whining?"

They shuffled, trying not to meet his eyes, and yet trying not to betray their comrade.

"I said, who's whining?" The overseer smiled, a savage twisting, of his lips utterly devoid of humour, and something animal-like and sub-human shone redly in his eyes. "So it's you, Carter, I might have guessed it." He jerked forward and grabbed the sobbing boy by the arm. "What's the matter, son?" he purred. "Did your mummy forget to tuck you in last night? Did your daddy forget to kiss you?" He laughed and, sycophantically, a few of the boys laughed with him.

They didn't mean to be deliberately cruel, but to them the concept of 'father' and 'mother' was utterly foreign. Most of them had been alone ever since they could remember and, unlike the sobbing boy who had only been orphaned a few months, to them the crude jest seemed meaningless.

"How old are you, son?" Still the mockery purred in the thick voice and Carter wiped his eyes as he stared up at the big man.

"Thirteen, sir."

"Almost a man aren't you? In a year or so you'll be inducted into the army, or you would have been if it hadn't been for that twisted spine of yours."

The big hand tightened on the frail arm. "You're not strong enough to work on the deadlands, son. You'd better come with me, I need a batman and I can use you. The last one died on me, fell over in the dark and broke his neck." The purr in the thick voice deepened. "You want to serve me, don't you?"

"I don't know, sir. I…"

"Do you want to work yourself to death, boy? Do you want to go as these others are going? You know what happens out there, you know how the radiations burn and blind, sear and distort. Be my batman, son, and you'll miss all that. Well?"

Carter licked his lips with a nervous gesture and stared appealingly at the blank faces around him.

He was a stranger, someone fresh from a life none of them had ever known, and they had long since learned the lesson of minding their own business.

They avoided his eyes.

"Yes, sir," he said helplessly. "I'll be your batman."

"Good." The overseer grinned and thrust the youth towards a huddle of low buildings. "Go and clear out my hut, you know where it is, and make a good job of it." He turned to the others. "Now you fatherless scum, get back to work, and work hard. If you don't…" He lifted his big fist and spat on the dirt at his feet. "I'll make you wish that you'd never been born."

He turned, walking with his jerking awkward stride towards the huddle of buildings, and silently the boys watched him go.

"The swine," said Wilson emotionlessly. "The dirty stinking swine!"

"Yeah." One of the others twisted his lips in contemptuous disgust. "I'll be glad to get the hell out of here. Nothing could be worse than this, not even the attack forces." He stared enviously at the blue-scarred boy. "You're lucky. Another year or so and you'll be old enough for the Fleet, they're taking them in at fourteen now I'm told."

"Maybe." Wilson shrugged and turned towards the mess hut. "The war may be over by then."

"It won't be," said the boy with quiet conviction, and shuddered as screams echoed thinly from the huddle of buildings. "The damn thing'll go on forever."

He was wrong.

Peace was declared two years later, signed and ratified over the smouldering ruins of the last desperate battle, and the Federation of Man was a cold fact. It had taken twenty years of constant struggle to weld the scattered colonies into a homogeneous whole, to break forever the stubborn pride of local groups and to end the inevitable threat of warring empires and divergent cultures. Now, after a generation, it had been accomplished, and the Federation of Man, born in hate and fear, in struggle and death, ruled the known stars.

There were splinter groups, of course, isolated planets with a single city and perhaps a few space ships, but they didn't count. What did count was the fact that the independent colonies now recognised the Mother Planet and acknowledged Earth as their nominal ruler, and, for the first time in a generation, men breathed the sweet air of freedom and the huge inter stellar ships traded once more between the stars.

Three years later, when Wilson was seventeen, the war was a thing of the past. Men streamed home and took up the reins of a disturbed existence, satisfied to farm and till, to work and build, their past forgotten, the ethics of the war, ignored, the long-term policy submerged in day to day interests.

Machines, turned from war-potential, cleared away the rubble and turned the revitalised soil. Cities reared towards the stars and the great warships lost their guns and atomic missiles, were ripped and altered, turned into harmless cargo vessels and passenger ships, sent to the outposts of the new Federation and once again all men were brothers.

Almost.

For still the unwanted remained, the children of war, the parentless, the waifs, the orphaned young and the footloose adventurers. They knew nothing these people, nothing but toil and the trade of death and in a peaceful world they were unwanted, unnecessary, and dangerous. So they were forgotten, ignored, their existence denied, shelved as an unfortunate problem which time would solve, and the new-born Federation unified itself and turned from war to peace with an energy born in dreams and a generation-long reaction from enforced discipline and conscription.

With peace came a revulsion of all things appertaining to war. The Terran fleet melted as its personnel dispersed, and men regained their personal liberty in a derision of all things military, so that a man in uniform became a thing of amused contempt, and the stiff discipline of armies a hateful burden.

Peace came.

CHAPTER 2

AN ADMIRAL SPEAKS

Three men sat in a luxurious room at the summit of the highest building in rebuilt London.

From high windows the dying light of the setting sun threw long streamers of red and gold, orange and pink, yellow and soft amber across the polished surface of a paper-littered table, reflecting in warm hues from the panelled walls. As the light died selenium controls clicked and subdued fluorescents restored the illumination.

Admiral Hogarth sighed and picked up a thin sheaf of papers from the pile before him. A tall man, his back die-straight and his thin shoulders square to his slender body, he fitted his neat uniform as though born to the black and gold.

Sparse white hair swept back from a high forehead and his eyes, pale, washed out blue, glittered from either side of a high-bridged, hooked nose beneath which his thin lips made a tight gash.

"It is decided then?" His voice was harsh, cold, emotionless and with the whip of ingrained command. "It is final?"

"It is." President Marrow looked at the third man. "Both Director Laurance and myself agree with the findings of the Committee and they are final. The Terran fleet is to be dispersed, the ships converted to commerce and the men and officers to have free choice either of continuing to operate the ships as civilian crews, or to be landed, free from military service, on any planet they may choose."

"You agree with this?" Hogarth stared at the fat Director and Laurance shrugged.

"Naturally."

"I see." The tall Admiral thinned his gash of a mouth. "And what are your plans concerning myself?"

"That," said the President quietly, "is the sole reason for this conference." He leaned back in his chair, an old man, tired, with the marks of ceaseless worry graven deep into his seemed features and his hairless scalp glistening in the soft lighting. "You present a problem, Hogarth, and I'm not attempting to deny it. For twenty years now you have had almost supreme power, in a way Earth owes you everything, for it was your fleet which smashed the Independents and established the Federation of Man, but that is over now, and frankly, we cannot afford nor tolerate a large military force."

"So you plan to leave yourselves defenceless?"

"Against what?" The President smiled and gently shook his head. "I understand you, Hogarth, please believe that, but you must accept the inevitable. Your fleet now has no further reason for existence, and with its passing..."

"I am an embarrassment." Hogarth nodded, his head dipping in a stiff, almost imperceptible salute. "I understand."

"I am glad that you do," murmured the President, and Laurance chuckled as he mopped his broad face with a square of gaily coloured linen.

"We'll find you a job, Admiral," he said cheerfully. "We don't know just what it will be yet, but there'll be something, you needn't worry."

"I'm not worried," said Hogarth tightly, "but you should be. What you propose is madness, sheer insanity, the abject logic of cowardice. You think that because the war is over you no longer have need of the space fleet. You are wrong. What of the insurgent worlds? What of the Raiders? What of the constant threat of rebellion?"

"Please." The President lifted one thin hand in a silent gesture. "Don't think us fools. We shall continue to operate a small armed force but it will be a local responsibility, a special police patrol more than anything else. We are talking now of the Terran Fleet, the mighty war engine you built and to operate which took the total resources of three worlds. That is finished, and, even if we wanted to keep it functioning, we couldn't do it."

"Why not?" Hogarth shrugged. "Because of the supply worlds?"

"No," said the old President gently, "because of the men."

"Nonsense!" For the first time the tall Admiral displayed emotion. "My men are loyal, they would fight and serve to the death, and…"

"Your men are deserting," interrupted Laurance impatiently. "While they were at war they would fight as you said, but not now, not now we are at peace and it's time to grow up."

"How dare you!"

"He's right, Hogarth," said the President wearily.

He sighed as he looked at the rigid figure of the Admiral, half-dreading what must be said and yet knowing that there was no alternative. A gigantic military machine had no place in the new Federation and both it and the men who ran it had to go. To retain it would be to strain the resources of too many worlds, occupy the valuable time of too many men, and always there would be the temptation of some highly placed officer to desert, to take a few ships, raid a planet for women and supplies, and head out into the depths of space, to the untouched stars waiting beyond the frontiers of the known worlds, and there establish a private empire.

It had happened before, half the Independent planets had been founded by exploiters and would-be dictators, and it had taken twenty years of savage fighting to break their local groups and to assimilate them into a homogeneous whole. It must not happen again.

Laurance was speaking, using the glib phrases of the born diplomat, and the old man listened to the honeyed words, knowing them for what they were, and yet hoping that the Admiral would take them at their face value. He hoped that Hogarth would, for the man still had power, still had control of a section of the Terran Fleet, and if he wanted to be awkward…

Apparently he didn't.

"I can follow your logic," he said stiffly, "but that doesn't mean I agree with it. Personally, I think that you are making a mistake, but you have the power, and you have the rule."

The old President frowned, half-catching the hint of mockery in the cold tones, but before he could speak Laurance had plunged ahead.

"…so you see, Hogarth there is nothing else we can do. The work of restoration simply does not permit of the drain necessitated by a large armed force, and it must be absorbed into the overall pattern. In fact we have already altered more than half the vessels and released most of the men and officers. All that remains now is to find you suitable employment, or if you would prefer retirement..."

He let his voice fade into a hopeful silence and for a moment the two men waited for the tall Admiral's reply.

"I do not wish to retire," he said coldly, and the fat man sighed in open disappointment.

"Then..."

"Before you decide," said Hogarth sharply, "May I speak?"

"Certainly."

"Thank you." This time there was no mistaking the irony in the tall man's cold voice. "I will not waste your time on further arguments on retaining the fleet, but there is a point which you seemed to have overlooked."

"Yes?" Laurance was still polite but his expression showed that he was getting fed up with all this and was eager to return to more constructive employment than persuading an unwanted Admiral that his time had passed.

"There is still need of a fighting force." Hogarth frowned at the fat man's instinctive gesture of annoyance. "Not, if you insist, from human enemies, but we have not explored the entire universe and it would be presumptuous for us to imagine that of all the worlds in the galaxy only our own has spawned life."

"We have found no other," said the President gently. He was an old man and could appreciate the other's battle to retain a shred of dignity and power.

"We have reached and covered an area of more than a hundred light years, but all the life we have found has been animal, unintelligent and relatively harmless."

"Does that mean we are alone?" Hogarth shook his head. "And what of opening new worlds and systems? Are we to send in colonising vessels filled with men and women to face an unknown environment? Is that to be the plan?"

Laurance didn't answer. He sat, his broad features pursed with thought, and his eyes as he stared at the tall Admiral were narrow with hidden speculation. He was no fool, a fool could never have risen to be one of the three Directors of the Federation of Man, and he sensed a hidden reason behind the seemingly innocent words. He decided to get to the point.

"What's on your mind, Hogarth?"

"I've told you."

"No, you haven't. You've spoken a lot of words, but what do they mean?" He glanced at a thin watch strapped to his pudgy arm. "I'll give you ten seconds to get to the point. After that you are automatically relieved of your rank and will be retired on full pay. Well?"

For a moment emotion showed through the ice and iron exterior of the tall Admiral. The pale, washed-out eyes glowed and the thin, cruel mouth thinned to a barely visible line. For perhaps five seconds he sat motionless, fighting an inner battle with his own emotions, then, calm returned and he smiled.

"You are astute, Laurance."

"Three seconds," snapped the Director. "Well?"

"I have a suggestion. It may appeal to you, and then again, it may not. Will you hear it?"

"More words?"

"Naturally. As I am not telepathic they are rather necessary, or is it too much to ask the Director to listen to the head of the armed forces which made his position possible?"

Laurance flushed, feeling the bite of the sarcasm, for, personal feelings aside, the cold fact remained that Hogarth had won the war. He swallowed, not daring to look at the old President, and nodded.

"Thank you." The tall man stared directly before him and when he spoke his voice was a cold whisper.

"I am a soldier, I have always been a soldier, ever since I entered the cadets at the age of fourteen, more than forty years ago now. I have been trained to handle men and machines, to plot and plan, to combine strategy and tactics, and the results of that training have placed you two gentlemen where you are. Now? Now it appears that I am finished, my skill unwanted, myself an embarrassment. I am to be retired, banished to some tiny world and there to end my life living with memories. I cannot do that. I will not do it!"

He blinked and his pale eyes gleamed like polished stone.

"You cannot banish me. You dare not. I am still head of the armed forces and there are still men to obey my commands. I refuse to be cast aside."

"Your men have deserted," reminded the old President gently. "And I cannot allow you to threaten the Federation of Man."

"I do not threaten—I beg." Hogarth swallowed and sweat glistened on his high forehead. "Is this to be my reward? I have fought for a generation to save what you have, am I to be thrown aside now that you have victory?"

"No, but what else can we do?" The President seemed genuinely troubled and he stared hopefully at the fat Director. Laurance shrugged, they had been over this problem a dozen times already and the answer always came out the same. One man against a system, and the man could not be allowed to win.

"Give me a small force," whispered Hogarth. "A few ships and a few men, some equipment and an unwanted planet for a base. Let me retain the trappings if not the power. Let me be the nucleus of an armed force should it ever be necessary."

"We have such a planet," mused the old man. "Stellar of the Capellian System, and we have the ships and some assorted supplies, but men..." He shrugged. "Who would volunteer for military duty now?"

"I can find them," said the tall Admiral quickly. "I…" He paused, staring at the expression on the fat Director's broad features. "What is it?"

"An idea," said Laurance slowly. He shook his head. "Sorry, I was thinking, but it wouldn't work. It couldn't."

"What couldn't?"

"You were speaking of men and the President said that no one would volunteer. He was wrong, there are some that would jump at the chance, but you'd never take them, you could never handle them if you did."

"No?" Hogarth frowned. "What men are you talking about?"

"Criminals," said Laurance flatly, and sat silent as his words faded into stillness.

"A prison planet?" Hogarth shook his head. "Is that all you can offer me?"

"It's that or nothing," said the fat man curtly. "The death penalty has been revoked beneath the new constitution, but we still have to find something to do with the prisoners. We know that forced labour takes more guards and produces less than paid. If you could take charge of them, make them work, train them…" He stared thoughtfully at the Admiral. "It is the obvious answer. We could grant you men and ships, guns and equipment. You would take the criminals, train them, use them to open new worlds, make them do something useful instead of letting them rot in some prison. Well?"

"I don't know," said Hogarth slowly. "How many men would there be?"

"Thousands, you'd be taking them all from the entire Federation, and most of the jails are full of unsettled criminals, returned soldiers, deserters, looters, the usual scum." He leaned across the polished table. "They are a headache to us, Hogarth. If you really want to do something useful, this is it. Stellar can become the penal world of the Federation, but it won't be easy and handling them will be hard."

"I can handle them," promised the tall man grimly. He hesitated. "I can count on a free hand?"

"How free?"

"Absolutely free. If I take on this task I must have no interference of any kind. You must send me what I need and I will take your unwanted scum and turn them into something useful. I want no humanists crying about harsh discipline, and I want all the men you can send me, all you decide are too much trouble for you to keep. Do you agree?"

"Yes," Laurance glanced at the old President.

"You needn't worry about interference, no one is going to worry over what happens to murdering scum and parasites on the body politic." He rose from the table and held out his hand. "When can you start?"

"Immediately. Stellar you say?"

"Yes."

"Stellar," murmured Hogarth, he seemed to savour the word. "In the Capellian System you say?"

"That's right." Laurance stared curiously at the tall man. "Do you know it?"

"No, but I assume that it is habitable?"

"Naturally."

"But harsh?"

"Of course, we could hardly spare a fertile world for use as a penal colony." The fat man stirred restlessly on his chair. "It's the best we can offer, Hogarth, the very best."

"It will do." The tall man smiled, his thin lips parting to show too-white teeth. "Thank you, gentlemen. If you will excuse me? There is much to do, but I will send you a list of my requirements in the morning and you may send me the first batch of prisoners within a month."

He bowed, a stiff-necked inclination of his head, and then he had gone, the panel sliding behind his angular figure as the elevator carried him down to the street level below. Laurance sighed and stared at the old President.

"It worked," he said with a hint of wonder in his smooth voice. "He accepted what we offered without argument."

"I'm glad," said the old man simply. "Hogarth is too valuable a man to be thrown aside, and if we did, he might prove dangerous."

"You think we can trust him now?"

"Of course. He is basically loyal and now he has work to do, men to lead, to train and command, and he will be happy. We can forget Hogarth, I have no doubts as to his real worth."

"And yet?" The fat man shook his head, half-annoyed at his own lack of conviction. "It seemed too smooth. Two problems solved at once, a man removed from a potentially dangerous position and our unwanted criminals trained and rehabilitated to be of use to the Federation in a normal life." He frowned. "Why should he have insisted on a free hand?"

"Why not?" The old President shrugged and scrawled a note on a sheaf of papers. "Hogarth is a martinet, a man who can give orders but who refuses to obey them. Forget him, there are other things to do, more important things than the disposal of an out-of-date military mind. Now. What are the food returns from the reclaimed areas?"

"As predicted," said the fat man absently. He stared at the wall, his broad features seamed with doubt, and his little eyes clouded with thought. Everything seemed to have gone as planned, the half-threat, the antagonism, the waiting for a suggestion, the forcing of a decision, then the appearance of acceptance and the making of conditions. It was elementary psychology, based on a shrewd knowledge of human nature and human weakness, a simple problem and one easily solved.

Too easily.

He wondered just who had been deluding whom.

CHAPTER 3

DUST

The soil was dry and gritty, reduced to a fine dust devoid of any trace of animal or vegetable matter, and holding within itself the seeds of ghastly death. In a sense it was ash, the residue of atomic war-dusts and the searing heat and radiation of liberated energy, dry and powdery, gritty and without cohesion, useless as a medium on which to grow as much as a blade of grass.

Wilson waved with his thick arm and a lumbering machine churned towards him on wide tracks. A wide-mouthed container jerked, settled, and thudded on the sterile soil and like automatons the group of boys and young men began to load it with hand shovels, filling it with poisoned dirt.

Around them dust plumed, covering their face plates and coating their thick protective clothing with a heavy layer of grey dirt. Within the suits heat made their flesh clammy with sweat, the oozing perspiration stinging their naked bodies, smarting as it trickled over ugly sores and chafed patches.

Above, high in a sky of clearest blue, the summer sun blasted them with added heat and made every move a torment of overstrained muscles and sweating exertion.

They had been working for five hours now, shovelling a foot deep layer of ruined topsoil into the mechanical containers, waiting for an empty bin to thud at their feet, filling it, waiting for another, filling it... It seemed to go on forever.

To either side of them, stretched all around the shrinking perimeter of the ruined area, other groups laboured beneath the sweltering sun, groups of ten, boys mostly, young men overseered by a veteran of the almost forgotten war, and working beneath the lash of frustration and sadistic hate.

For these unwanted waifs of the war there had been no peace.

Wilson paused, leaning on his shovel and easing the ache in his throbbing back. Next to him a short, stunted, almost monkey-like youth of perhaps sixteen, swore, flung down his shovel, and threw back his thick hood.

"To hell with it," he spat. "I've had enough."

"Replace your hood," snapped Wilson, his voice distorted as it vibrated from the diaphragm. "You want to go blind?"

"I won't go blind," protested the short youth, but he replaced his hood and stood, wide-legged, staring out across the seared desert. "Why don't they give us mechanical shovels? Why don't they use bulldozers, grabs, tractor power? We could clean this area up in a couple of months if we had the tools but instead of that we've got to pick up every damn grain by hand. I'll take years at this rate."

"Maybe they haven't got any machines."

"They've got 'em right enough. I know. I was working up north before I came here, on the Cumberland area, and we had full equipment, shovels, bulldozers, everything." He snorted and kicked at the dust. "You know what I think? I don't reckon they want us to finish this job. You know why? Because they want somewhere to put us, that's why, and shovelling dirt is as good a way as any to keep us quiet."

"Why should they want to keep us quiet?"

"Don't you know?" The short youth lifted his hood and spat on the dust. "I got sent here because I'd been a bad boy." Mockery tinged his cynical voice. "The police grabbed me when I tried to break in a warehouse, and they sent me to Cumberland. I tangled with an overseer there, some character who wanted me to be his batman." He made an obscene noise. "I looked after him all right. They had to put the guy in hospital and they shipped me out fast. I…"

"Wait!" Wilson stared at the wrinkled features peering at him from behind the faceplate. "You said the police picked you up?"

"That's right."

"Then you haven't always been working in a party."

"Who said I had? My people died a couple of years ago and I dodged loose for a while. That's when I got arrested." He stared curiously at the blue-scarred young man. "What's the matter, Wilson? You look queer."

"Forget it." The young man stooped over his shovel and threw dirt into the waiting container.

Externally he seemed as always but inside him, deep within the confines of his skull, thoughts chased each other like rats in an elaborate maze.

For the first time he realised that he had been forgotten in the tides of restoration.

His education had been scanty, he could read, write, and, thanks to a course of hypno-tuition, he had a smattering of common knowledge, but the main source of his education had been in studying his fellow unfortunates. Of the outside world, of the peace, the concept of personal liberty, the right of man to live in his own way and to make his own destiny, he had no knowledge. He had thought, there had been no reason for thinking otherwise, that life as he knew it was common to all.

Now...

Now he learned of something new, a different set of data on which to base assumptions. The short man had spoken of machines, of police, of a life in which some degree of freedom was obviously possible. He'd had, to a limited degree perhaps, a free choice. He was here because he had committed a crime, more than one if his story about the overseer was true, and that meant...

Wilson felt sick anger clog his throat and fill his stomach with the warm knots of hate.

The short youth was a criminal. He was not.

Why then should they do the same work, live the same life, share the same things? One was here from choice, the other from circumstances over which he'd had no control, and, as he thought about it, Wilson's grey eyes narrowed and his scarred cheek twitched.

For the very first time in his seventeen years of existence he felt a sense of injustice.

They worked steadily for another hour, then, climbing aboard a swaying, flat-bottomed turbine truck, jolted towards the mess huts a couple of miles from the site of operations. An air hose blew the contaminated dust from their protective clothing, and, throwing back the hoods, they sat down at the rough tables at their food.

During the meal, the usual mess of yeast products, dehydrated vegetable matter and soya bean flour, silence filled the hut, a silence broken only by the rattle of spoons and the half-animal slobbering of half-starved youths gulping at their food. Then, when the last plate had been wiped dry, they relaxed for the fifteen minutes remaining of the meal break. A pale boy, not more than thirteen, wiped sweat from his face and stared sickly at Wilson.

"I don't feel so good," he said. "I've got cramps and my stomach hurts."

"Take some salt pills."

"I have, they don't make any difference."

"Well, what do you want me to do about it?" Wilson stared at the boy. "If you're sick, report to the overseer, but make sure that you're sick first."

"I'm sick."

"Then what are you waiting for?" Wilson jerked his head toward the upper table at which the overseers ate. "Hoppy's up there, go and see him now, and if he says so you can lay up this afternoon."

The boy nodded and, rising from the table, went up to the overseer. The man glared at him, suffering torment this hot weather from the pain of his ill-fitting artificial legs.

"What do you want?"

"I feel sick, sir. Wilson said that if you give permission I can rest this afternoon."

"He did, did he?" The big man glowered at the pale face of the scarred youth. "Since when have you given the orders around here, Wilson?" He didn't trouble to lower his voice and silence fell as the rest of the men and boys looked on.

"I gave no orders—sir, I told him to see you."

"Why?"

"He said that he feels sick, could be heat prostration, or something he ate. In any case a sick boy is useless out on the site."

"Getting soft, Wilson?"

The young man shrugged, not bothering to argue with a man for whom he felt disgusted contempt.

The overseer sensed his emotion and anger twisted his mouth into an ugly snarl.

"Since you feel so sorry for him you can couple up with him for the next three shifts. If you want to give him a rest you can do his work, and remember this, Wilson, if you don't fill the quota you'll be sorry for it."

"Like Carter was sorry?" Wilson stared at the convulsed features of the big man. "He's dead now, isn't he? I remember hearing him scream the night he was supposed to have cut his throat. I…"

"Shut your mouth!" The overseer rose from the table with such force that his chair skidded across the uneven floor and slammed against the wall. "That was a year ago now."

"Yes," said the young man quietly. "A year ago, and ever since then you've had to clean up your own hut." He stared deliberately at the big man. "I wonder why, Hoppy?"

"Don't call me that you…" Filth streamed from the big man's lips and he lunged forward, forgetting in the heat of his anger the limitations of his artificial legs. He stumbled, staggered, and fell, his face hitting the edge of the table with the sound of bone striking wood, and when he climbed slowly to his feet his face was masked with the blood which rilled from his broken nose.

Wilson laughed.

He regretted it almost at once, regretted the insane, frustrated anger which made him hold the man up to ridicule, but it was too late and, as the overseer stumbled towards the door, he felt his flesh cringe beneath a murderous look of vindictive hate.

"You've done it now," whistled the short, monkey-like youth at his side. "He's out to get you, Wilson, get you for sure."

"Perhaps."

"There's no 'perhaps' about it. I know. I've seen that look before." He stared calculatingly at the young man. "Are you going to get him first?"

"Murder him you mean?"

"You could call it that." The youth shrugged. "Me, I prefer to call it insurance, but suit yourself. Are you?"

"He'll calm down," said Wilson uneasily. "He may ride me hard for a while but I can stand it."

"What's the matter, can't you face the truth?" The short youth grunted. "I tell you that he'll get you if it's the last thing he does. He can't do otherwise, you laughed at him, made him look a fool, and worse than that, he guesses that you know something about him. I know what I'd do in his place and he don't look the type of man who needs any lessons."

"Forget it," said Wilson uncomfortably. "Let's get back to work."

"What about the sick guy?"

"He comes with us." Wilson rose from the table and led the group out to the waiting vehicle. Back on the site he grabbed a shovel and began working like a man possessed, trying to do a double quota to cover up for the boy who lay, groaning from internal misery, on the gritty, radioactive soil. The short man watched him, grinning with amused contempt, and when he spoke his distorted voice held undisguised contempt.

"What are you trying to do, kill yourself?"

"No." Wilson grunted as he flung dirt into the huge container. "I'm covering up for the sick boy, if we don't fill our quota the overseer will half skin us."

"Why take the rap for someone else?" The short youth leaned idly on his shovel. "Anyway, you're in so bad a little more can't make any difference. Why not take it easy?"

"No, I..." Wilson paused, the shovel dropping from his gloved hands, and dust plumed beneath his feet as he flung himself forward. "You crazy fool!" he snapped. "Get that hood back on. Quick!"

"I can't!" The sick boy stared up from where he writhed on the poisoned soil, and against his pale, sweat-streaked features, his wide dark eyes seemed like twin pools of ebon agony. "I'm burning. I can't breathe and I want to be sick."

"Then be sick," snapped Wilson curtly. "Bring your heart up if you feel like it, but get that hood back on first."

"I..." The boy gulped and saliva trickled from the corners of his mouth. "I..." He retched, shuddering as he vomited the contents of his stomach onto the gritty dust. He twisted, blind with pain and forgetting everything but the burning agony tearing at his fever-wracked body. He rolled—and buried his face in the radioactive soil.

For a moment neither of the two youths moved or spoke, then Wilson had dropped to his knees and, gripping the boy by the shoulders, lifted and turned him with a savage burst of energy. Carefully he brushed the grey dust from the pale features, wincing as he saw the tell-tale specks of dirt black against the white of the staring eyeballs. Behind him the short youth sucked in his breath, and, lifting his hood, spat on the dust.

"That's it," he said grimly. "For him it's lights out."

"We've got to get him back to the hospital hut."

Wilson stared up at the short youth. "You take him, tell the driver of the turbine truck what happened, and he'll give you a lift." He snarled as the short youth made no effort to relieve him of his burden. "Damn you, didn't you hear me? Hurry. There may still be a chance of saving his eyes."

"If you say so." The youth grunted as he gripped the moaning figure and flung the slight body over his shoulders. "Personally, I think you're wasting time. Why not leave him here? Do you think he'll thank you for saving his life and not his eyes? Get wise, Wilson. With that dust in his eyes he hasn't a chance and you know it."

"Get moving, damn you! He might be lucky, but while you stand yapping he's getting worse." He stepped forward and something in his cold grey eyes made the short youth step hurriedly backwards.

"Well?"

"I'm going," gasped the short, monkey-like youth. "I'm going now." Dust plumed from beneath his feet as he half-ran towards the waiting vehicle five hundred yards away.

Sickly Wilson picked up his shovel and returned to work.

He knew that the boy didn't stand a chance of retaining his sight. He had seen too many accidents to be deluded for a minute, but, despite his inner conviction, the attempt had to be made. A puff of wind could do it, a single speck of the radiant soil, lodging in an eye and searing the delicate tissues with its invisible death. First would come a soreness, an irritation, a red inflammation spreading across the ball and clouding the pupil. Then would come the open sore, the un-healable wound running with continual pus, the breakdown of living tissue, and it would eat deeper and deeper and deeper…

Usually they had to remove the eye.

He shook his head, half annoyed with himself for feeling so deeply over the troubles of someone who meant nothing to him, and dust swirled from beneath his shovel as he tried to relieve his emotions in arduous labour. He worked until he could hardly see through the dust covered face plate, worked until the sweat trickled in great streams over his soggy flesh, worked until his muscles ached and he reeled on the edge of heat prostration, and still an image painted itself on the inner wall of his mental vision, the image of a young boy, hardly thirteen, blind and helpless in a world in which he wasn't wanted.

Blind through no fault of his own.

He paused at last, sucking great breaths of filtered air and fighting the temptation to remove his hood and feel the warm air against his streaming face. Clumsily he wiped the face plate, dragging the back of his glove over the scratched plastic, then, after a long moment, reached for his shovel.

It wasn't there.

He reached again, swinging his hand in a wide arc behind him, where he had thrust it in a mound of soil. Still nothing, and he turned, half angry, half puzzled to look for the tool.

A man grinned at him from behind a wide faceplate, a big man with a shovel in his hand and blood streaked features. A man with a broken nose.

The overseer.

CHAPTER 4

DUEL OF DEATH

For a moment neither of them moved, then Wilson turned, narrowing his eyes as he stared at the emptiness around them, looking for the other members of his group.

"They're gone," said the big man softly. "I sent them away. We're all alone here, Wilson, all alone."

"So I see." The young man held out his hand.

"If you'll give me the shovel I'll get back to work."

"Forgetting something, Wilson?"

"I'm sorry—sir. But I have a quota to fill and I can't work without a shovel."

"Yes, your quota." The overseer stared at the half-filled container. "You must have lost track of the time. Where are the other two?"

"The boy fell sick, ripped off his hood and got dust in his eyes. I sent him back to the hospital huts and a man to go with him."

"Dust in his eyes, eh? That's bad. Very bad." There was a false concern in the big man's voice that made the young man writhe. A syrupy, artificial emotion, in which the man's innate sadism seemed to relish the thought of suffering and pain. Wilson stared at him, feeling his stomach muscles tighten and his heart accelerate from released adrenaline triggered by the twin emotions of hate and fear.

"Is work finished for the day, sir?" He fought to keep his voice even, knowing that any display of fear would only spur the man on to brutality, and yet trying to remain polite so as not to give an excuse for violence. The big man grinned, his mouth twisting into an animal-snarl utterly devoid of humour and heavy with anticipation.

"Yes."

"Then shall we go back, sir?"

"In a hurry, Wilson?"

"No, sir, but it's hot and I'd like a shower."

"A shower?" The big man took a stride forward, his artificial legs jerking as they dragged at the hampering dust. Wilson watched him, his grey eyes flickering from the blood-smeared features to the hand gripping the shovel, the tool looking frail and light in the big paw.

"Yes, sir. A shower."

The overseer didn't reply, but stood, swaying a little, his feet shifting as they steadied his weight.

"You broke my nose, Wilson," he said abruptly. "You laughed at me. I don't like to be laughed at, Wilson. I don't like it one little bit."

"No, sir," said the young man mechanically. "Sorry, sir." He licked his lips, and his grey eyes continued to flick from the shovel to the staring eyes, from the eyes to the shovel. He was afraid. He knew it, knew it from the sweat trickling down his face and back, and from the way his heart hammered against his ribs, and instinctively he cringed, the conditioning of seventeen years taking charge and turning his strength to water. The overseer was the boss and the boss was always right The boss had always been right and, reared as he had been in the iron grip of emotionless authority, he had a terrible fear of those in command.

Now that fear threatened his life.

"I hate you, Wilson," said the big man thickly. "I've always hated you. I don't like your eyes, your hair, and I don't like the blue scar on your face. I know you and I know your sort. Troublemakers, that's what you are, and you broke my nose."

"I'm sorry about that, sir," stammered Wilson desperately. "I…"

Almost he was too late. Almost he had relaxed too far, tried the known weapons of fawning politeness against the safer ones of action. A gleam of light saved him, the reflected light from the setting sun as it glanced off the polished surface of the shovel blade, and he ducked, dropping to the dust as the thrown tool sliced through the air where his head had been.

Even then he didn't move, he couldn't, fear of authority and fear of what would happen should he dare to strike the overseer numbed him and chilled his blood. Sickly he watched the big man march forward, dragging his metal limbs' painfully across the dust. He stopped and when he rose the shovel gleamed against the sinking sun, reed-like in the big hand.

"I'm going to kill you, Wilson," he said thickly. "You know that, don't you?"

"No, sir." The young man trembled as he stared at the overseer. "Why, sir?"

"Does that matter?" Insane merriment quivered in the heavy voice. "Do you want to live, you swine? Do you?"

"Yes, sir."

"Then take off your hood. Take it off I say before I split your skull!"

Wilson hesitated, staring over the emptiness around them, desperately hoping that someone would come, some other overseer, a boy worker e even, anyone to make the madman stop and think of what he was doing.

"You can't kill me," he panted. "You can't! I'll be missed. I..."

"Take off that hood!" The overseer lurched forward, the upraised shovel glinting in his hand. "Take it off!"

"Why—sir?"

"Why?" The big man grinned, his lips writhing from broken teeth and the dried blood on his battered features cracking in the semblance of a grotesque mask. "You whining dog! You see too much and know too much. I can cure that. Take off your hood—and roll in the dust!"

"No!" Wilson stepped back, swallowing the mounting horror threatening to choke him. He thought of the things he had seen, the terrible sores caused by the radioactive dust, and a face floated before his mental vision, a noseless, eyeless, , obscenely disfigured face. His own! Death swept at him, the sharp edged shovel glinting as it swung like some ancient battleaxe towards his head.

He dropped, feeling his left arm go numb as the shovel slashed at his thick protective clothing. The overseer swore, lurched forward, and the shovel whined as it slashed through the air. It whined, swinging in a wide arc, and the force of the blow twisted the big man on his metal legs, the pain from his chafed stumps spilling in savage curses from between his twisted lips.

Wilson stared up from where he cowered in the dust and knew with cold certainty that he could never survive a third attack. He rolled, his long legs threshing at the gritty soil, and dust plumed in a fine cloud, masking the sun, and turning the bulky figure of the big man into something half-seen, monstrous, almost unreal. Beneath the cover of that dust he moved with a frantic, half-animal reaction to urgent danger.

He kicked, missed, kicked again, and, even as the blade of the shovel thudded flatly against his skull, his heel drove against the overseer's metal knee.

Pain filled him, the sick pain of semi-concussion, and flecks of black and red danced across his dimming vision. Desperately he struggled to retain awareness and blood ran from his bitten lips as he pitted pain against pain, conscious that if he flagged now, he was as good as dead. Crouching on the dust he stared through the fogged faceplate and dragged his glove over the dust-covered surface.

Before him the big man stood, stork-like, one of his metal limbs functioning as normal, the other broken by the savage kick, the knee joint smashed and fixed into rigidity. Even as he watched, the big man flung himself forward, hands outstretched and his snarling face looking tiger-like as he reached for the young man's throat.

Dust climbed towards the fading light of the heavens as they fought.

Wilson was young but all his life he had known nothing but toil, and his figure, slight though it was, held a hidden strength. His muscles were long, stringy, and his sinews had been toughened by moving tons of rubble and countless tons of poisoned soil. What he lacked in weight he gained in litheness and he wriggled like an eel beneath the crushing weight of the big man.

Hands tore at his hood, an elbow thrust at the pit of his stomach and another jabbed at his throat. He twisted, bringing up his knee, ripping the destroying hands from his hood, panting, wasting more energy in a futile effort to escape and even now half afraid of attacking the big man. He retched as an elbow jabbed hard into his stomach, and gasped as the edge of a stiffened palm slashed across his throat, tasting blood from his damaged tissues. The blow weakened him, and, as he collapsed on the dirt, the big man flung himself forward and his heavy body crushed the slight young man hard against the soil.

He laughed, thick, sadistic laughter, and his gloved hands fumbled at the fastenings of Wilson's hood.

"You see too much," he slobbered. "You know too much, but I can cure that. I'm not going to kill you, I don't have to, the dust can do it for me. There's going to be an accident, a bad accident, and I'll drag you back to the hospital huts for treatment." He laughed again. "Who's going to blame me if you were fool enough to take off your hood and fall against the dust? Some of you scum get contaminated every day, and who's going to worry about a fatherless swine?"

He grunted as the hood came loose.

Terror flamed through the numbed tissues of the young man, the mad, half-crazed terror of anticipation and knowledge of what the overseer intended and with the terror came the strength of desperation. He twisted, forcing himself away from the fumbling hands, and the big man snarled as he tried to surge forward, his useless metal limb hampering, hanging like a leaden weight from his sore stump, the connections dragging at his nerves.

He grunted, clenching his big fist and hammering at the young man's faceplate, starring the scratched glass in an effort to rupture the helmet and fill it with the poisoned soil. He swore, his mouth twisted into an animal-snarl, and Wilson knew that any appeal to mercy or justice would be a waste of time.

He writhed, twisting with frantic strength, jerking his knees hard against the gross body, thrusting with his gloved hands, kicking with long legs as he struggled to free himself from the crushing weight of the big man's body.

He wriggled, rolled, dust pluming around them like a thick cloud as he crawled desperately away.

A hand gripped his ankle and he kicked at it, lashing out with his heavy boot, fighting like a cat with hands and feet, rolling over onto his back as he fought. Glass shattered beneath his heel and he kicked again, unthinkingly, desperately, and dirt showered from beneath his boot, a thick mass of gritty soil, dashing against the broken faceplate and filling the ruptured helmet with invisible death.

The overseer screamed!

He shrieked, rolling in agony on the dirt, the battle forgotten as he tried to gouge his eyes free of the contaminated grit. Desperately he ripped off his hood, tore off his heavy gloves, spat dirt from between his lips as he clawed at his eyes and from his open mouth spilled a low, animal-like whimper of horrified sound.

"My eyes!" he shrieked. "My eyes! Oh, God, my eyes!"

Wilson stared at him, sick with horror at what he had done, and, as he rose to his feet and staggered backwards, his foot struck against the discarded shovel. Automatically he picked it up.

"Help me," whimpered the overseer. "I can't see! I'm blind! Blind! Help me, damn you! For God's sake help me!"

He groped before him, blindly, his stiffened leg trailing like the broken limb of a crippled spider as he crawled over the dirt. One big hand touched Wilson's ankle, and it fastened there, huge and strong and utterly terrible.

"Got you!" Insane triumph quivered in the thick voice. "You've blinded me, you swine! You've blinded me! But I'll get even. I'll pull you down and gouge out your eyes. I'll rip out your tongue and tear off your ears. I'll…" The big hand jerked and Wilson staggered beneath the incredible strength of the insane creature at his feet.

What happened then was born from mercy and fear. Mercy springing from the knowledge of what must inevitably happen to the contaminated overseer, and fear of what would happen if he did not act. Mingled with the fear was hate, and both hate and fear complimented each other, building as a harmonic resonance would build, rising to a nerve-tearing crescendo aided and dominated by the thing at his feet.

The shovel lifted and swung, the bright blade gleaming in the dying light of the summer sun, whining through the air from the force of its passage. Once, twice, three times it struck and the blade was no longer bright and silence fell over the man-made desert, silence broken only by the steady drip, drip, drip, of falling blood.

From the distant huts the tiny figures of men grew, limned against the dying light as they made their way across the grey plain, heading towards the spot where he stood.

Waiting.

CHAPTER 5

OBEY AND SURVIVE

Admiral Hogarth sat in his office and stared through high windows at his new domain. Stellar was a 'heavy' planet with a gravity almost twice that of Earth, but despite the drag he sat as straight as ever, his thin shoulders rigid beneath the thin material of his uniform. Now he no longer wore the proud black and gold of the Terran Fleet, but a simpler uniform of neutral grey against which the scarlet of his insignia showed like splotches of newly shed blood.

A grim place this penal world, more than fifty light years from Earth and blasted by a sun nearly two hundred times as fierce as the Solar Furnace. It was an old world, its seas evaporated and its rotation slowed so that it turned once on its axis each year, and so it kept one face permanently facing the searing brightness of Capella while the other looked eternally at the glowing stars.

It had air, near enough to that of Earth to be breathable, and the temperature difference between day and nightside formed convection currents that swept the planet in predictable winds, and, because of those winds, life was tolerable on a wide strip circumnavigating the globe, a twenty mile strip known as the twilight belt.

It was a harsh world, a world of desert and ice, of heat blistered sand and frozen soil, a contrast of extremes, rough, crude, un-softened by the hand of man, a forlorn planet bypassed in the rush to colonise more fertile and gentler worlds.

But Hogarth was satisfied, and, as he stared at the bleak terrain, something glowed for a moment in his pale blue eyes, and his thin shoulders stiffened a fraction of a millimeter more beneath his impeccable uniform. . .

On the wide desk before him an intercom hummed its muted attention signal.

"Yes?"

"The new intake has arrived, sir. Normal procedure?"

"Yes."

"Very good, air. Five minutes?"

"That will do." Hogarth broke the connection and rose to his feet. From a rack he took his visored cap, stiff with scarlet braid, and, after a moment's hesitation, replaced a wide belt heavy with holstered weapons. He glanced at himself in a mirror, then, satisfied with his appearance, left the room.

His aide waited for him in the corridor, a short, scar-faced man, his grey uniform rumpled and his captain's insignia faded. He wore twin pistols at his waist and high on one cheek a muscle twitched in uncontrollable nervous reaction. Hogarth nodded towards him and the short man fell into step at his side.

"How many this time, Captain?"

"Fifty, sir."

"Is that all?" Hogarth frowned. "I had expected more."

"It's just as well there are only fifty, sir." The stocky captain gnawed at his lower lip. "Until we can train men to augment the guards I shan't feel easy. Personally I haven't slept a whole night through since we landed here, and neither have the others."

"I see, but you knew what to expect, Captain."

"I know, sir, and I'm not grumbling, but the strain is beginning to tell. We should have started with more guards, sir. Either that or less prisoners."

"Do others feel the same way about it as you do?"

"I think so, sir." The short man glanced up at the tall Admiral. "Not that we are grumbling you realise, sir, but it is as well that you know these things."

"I understand, Captain," said Hogarth quietly. "We shall speak of it later."

He blinked as they left the coolness of the building and stepped into the hot sun. Grouped at a little distance from the building a cluster of men lounged in various attitudes on the gritty sand, some lying on their backs, others sitting, the rest lying on their sides, but all resting their bodies from the gravity drag. Guards stood around them, hard-eyed, hard-faced men, and the bright sunlight glittered from the barrels of sub-guns and rifles, scintillated from a squat, long barrelled semi-portable Nione, and bathed each man's face with glistening sweat.

Hogarth halted and the stocky captain strode towards the lounging men.

"On your feet," he rapped. "At the double now. Move!"

They stared at him, not moving, the scum of a dozen worlds, killers, men who had expected death and were ready for it, and, as they lounged and stared, tension mounted, a strained conflict of wills, one against fifty.

The captain didn't argue. He lifted his left arm, moving it in a swift gesture, and sunlight shimmered from the long barrel of the Nione, as it lifted, pointing above the heads of the clustered men.

Fire streamed from it, fire and the thundering report of riven air as the disrupted particles of exploded atoms tore a passage through the heavy atmosphere. For a split second of time a shaft of searing brilliance shamed the bright light of the swollen sun, then it vanished, the sound died to murmuring echoes and in the shocked silence the captain's voice rapped with fresh authority.

"The next blast incinerates the lot of you. Now. On your feet!"

They moved then, snarling and muttering curses as they lifted themselves against the double gravity.

They rose and stood, listless, arms hanging loosely at their sides, their shoulders rounded and their heads hanging on their chests beneath the cruel weight of their own bone and flesh.

"Stand to attention! Straighten those backs, lift those chins, pull in those stomachs. Move. Move or by all the Gods of Space I'll flay you alive!"

Sullenly they obeyed the harsh voice, the glinting barrel of the semi-portable a grim reminder of what they were and what could happen to them. Dust swirled beneath their feet as they shuffled into some sort of line, and mouths twisted to obscene curses as men who had never tried to stand correctly before in their entire lives, forced sagging muscles to protesting obedience.

The stocky captain glared at them, his thin mouth twisted in disgust, then grunted, turned on his heel, and snapped a sharp salute at the waiting Admiral.

"Ready for inspection, sir."

Hogarth nodded and strode towards the ranks of waiting men.

Idly he scanned them, letting his cold eyes drift over the faces of the convicted prisoners. Old men, young men, men with the stamp of dissipation and the animal-like lack of self-control. Drug addicts and drunkards, tramps and fallen angels, natural-born criminals and the unfortunate victims of circumstances beyond their control. Men from a dozen star systems and a score of worlds. Men with black hair and blond, red hair and grey, white hair and no hair at all. Clear-eyed men and men with the yellow eyeballs and muddy pupils of ill-living and degeneracy. Fifty of them, all unwanted, all failures, all sent here for training and rehabilitation.

All killers.

Once he paused, letting his pale, washed out eyes rest on a young man, a pale-faced youth still in his teens, a boy with an ugly patch of blue scarring the left side of his neck and face. For a moment he looked at him, noting the clear grey eyes and the straight back, the black hair and the thin mouth, then he continued his examination, his harsh features betraying no emotion.

For a long time he kept them waiting, moving slowly up and down the sagging line, his eyes like twin jewels in the shadow of his visored cap, then he stepped back, and, clasping his hands behind him rocked gently on his parted feet.

"Men," he said abruptly. "You are on Stellar. You have been sent here because you are murderers, unwanted, the scum of the Federation. Within four months half of you will be dead, within eight, two thirds, and if ten of you are still alive at the end of a year I shall be more than satisfied for those ten will be—men!" He paused, a calculated pause, waiting for the sense of his words to resister with the new arrivals. One or two of them straightened, staring at him with startled wonder, and his thin lips twisted in an ironical smile.

"You have but one duty here. One order you must never forget. You must obey. You must obey any order given you by any uniformed guard, any order given you by any officer, obey instantly and without question. Obey! Remember that." He paused again and when he spoke his voice was as hard and cold as ice and iron. "We have but one penalty on Stellar. One punishment for those who refuse to fall in line. Death. You obey, or you die" Remember that!"

He nodded towards the sweating captain and the stocky man rapped swift orders.

"Attention!" Stiffly he saluted the Admiral. "Permission to dismiss, sir?"

"Permission granted."

The captain saluted again and turned to face the collapsing line of new arrivals.

"Left turn! Quick march! One, two, three, keep in line there!"

They shuffled away, their feet dragging at the gritty sand, and with them went the armed guards, two of them carrying the semi-portable. Hogarth watched them file towards the low huts of the living quarters, some of the older men almost falling as they reached the shelters, and other men, earlier arrivals on the penal world, paused from their labours to stare at them with hard-eyed interest.

Hogarth smiled, a thin, mirthless twisting of his cruel mouth, and, flicking a speck of dust from his uniform, strode towards the Admin building.

Later, when 'night' as they still called a ten hour division of the twenty hour 'day', had fallen, the tall Admiral called a conference in his private office. The sun still seared the arid desert, the continual winds still circulated softly over the planet, sweeping high above as the cold air from the night-side was warmed and expanded, rising to make room for more cold air. But now the settlement was deserted, the living quarters locked, and, aside from a few patrolling guards, the entire area had a lifeless, desolate look as if man had touched there but briefly and had long since gone.

Hogarth stared at his officers, the select few who were permitted to question his decrees and who knew his overall plans, his apparent plans that is, for none of them even pretended to guess at the secret thoughts living behind the pale, washed out blue of the cold eyes. There was the stocky captain, the doctor, the psychologist, and two other officers, all with the hard faces and ruthless eyes of men who have seen much and whose dreams were not bound by common barriers. These, together with some fifty others, consisted of the entire force of the penal colony and for a man who had commanded the thousand ships and million men of the armed forces of Terra, it was small consolation.

Hogarth cleared his throat as they sat around the wide desk, and sat for a moment, his cold eyes flickering from face to face.

"Captain Rennie informs me that some of you have doubts," he said evenly. "Is this so?"

"Doubts?" The doctor shrugged. "No doubts, Hogarth, certainty. Fifty men, even though armed as ours are, cannot control hundreds of desperate prisoners for long. It is a matter of predictable breakdown." He glanced at the psychologist. "Am I correct, Dewer?"

"You are," snapped the psychologist. He was a little man, old, and with an expression of perpetual irritation. "I have plotted a graph and I can state that mutiny and riot will occur within six months at the present rate of intake. A point will be reached when we either arm some of the prisoners to augment the guards, or be swamped by sheer weight of numbers." He shrugged. "I don't have to tell you of the danger of the first alternative."

"To arm the prisoners would be suicidal," snapped one of the other two captains. He flushed as the tall Admiral gestured for silence.

"Your predictions are based on continuance of present policy?"

"Yes," snapped the psychologist.

"I see." Hogarth nodded and his cold eyes seemed infused with a secret amusement. "Naturally, I am aware of the danger, but believe me, gentlemen, it is not my intention to allow matters to reach such a critical point."

"I knew it," chuckled the stocky captain. "You have a plan, sir?"

"Yes," said the tall man quietly. "I have a plan." He paused, staring at the bleak desert outside of the high windows, and when he spoke his voice held a peculiar dream-like quality as though he spoke more to himself than to those around him.

"Fifty-six men," he whispered. "Hard men, men who are used to discipline and who know how to obey. The very best men I could find for my purpose, the cream of my loyal command men whom I must trust—or kill!" He ignored the stir of shocked surprise as his listeners shifted uncomfortably on their hard chairs.

"We have a planet here, arms equipment, our own spaceship and a free hand. We have men, killers, scum, the unwanted rabble of the nice clean Federation, and they ask us to turn filth into something to be proud of. Two hundred prisoners at the moment and more to come, many more, thousands more, a continual stream as the prisons are emptied and the cities swept and purified of their sulking murderers. Raw material to be shaped as we wish. Hard and ruthless men to be fashioned to fit the moulds of our own making, and they are mine, all mine, body and soul!"

He blinked and some of the glaze left his eyes as he stared at the watching faces of the waiting men.

"Naturally we can't guard them forever, and equally naturally we daren't arm them as they are, but there is an alternative."

"Yes?" The little psychologist leaned forward, his thin features alive with interest. "How?"

"By turning scum into men, prisoners into soldiers, filth into cream." Hogarth leaned back in his chair. "We shall found a new Legion, and, as we are on a planet of that name, we shall call it the Stellar Legion. We have the raw material, we have the knowledge, and we have the power. We shall train the broken fools they send us, train them as men have never been trained before, and when we have finished with them, we shall have all the guards we need, all the servants we can use, all the power we shall want. Think of it, gentlemen. A new fighting force, a tough, hard, ruthless group of men who have been taught and trained to the last degree. The Stellar Legion!"

Silence fell as his words faded against the walls, and the men stared at each other, each busy with his own thoughts. It was the stocky captain who broke the growing tension.

"Can we do it, sir? What of Earth, the Federation, will they allow us to build a fighting force?"

"They gave me a free hand," said Hogarth tersely. "In any case, can you suggest an alternative method of controlling the prisoners?"

"No, sir."

"How are you going to train them?" The doctor leaned forward, his eyes narrowed, and deep lines running from nose to the corners of his sensual mouth. "This is a heavy planet, remember, and most of the prisoners are far from fit."

"Their health is your concern, doctor, the training methods are mine and Dewer's." He glanced at the little psychologist. "First, they must be acclimatised to conditions here. You know your own business, doctor, but I would suggest heavy injections of ultra-calcium, a diet rich in protein and vitamin content, and the use of whatever drugs and injections you see fit to restore them to health. I can give you a month with each new batch. Those obviously incapable of arduous training can be retained for fatigue duties. All the others must have a rigorous course of calisthenics and exercises aimed at developing muscle and general health."

"I can do that," mused the doctor. "I have ideas as how to use several of the new synthetic drugs." He glanced at the tall Admiral. "Many of the prisoners are drug addicts, some have organic disease, others are basically weak through malnutrition and neglect. Do I treat them all with full care or concentrate on those who can benefit from treatment?"

"I see that you begin to understand me, doctor." Hogarth gave one of his rare smiles. "Those who are on the brink of death would be an unnecessary burden. How you restore their health is solely your concern, but remember, one month only for each batch." He paused. "I think that it would be as well for you to know that I am not concerned with the death rate. All I am interested in is fit material for future training. Need I say more?"

"No, sir." The doctor smiled and leaned back in his chair, his eyes narrowed and cloudy with thought, a peculiar half-smile on his sensuous lips.

"As from now all captains must give strict orders that the slightest sign of hesitation or disobedience in obeying an order must be punished by instant death. The sentence to be carried out immediately and in front of the offender's fellows." Hogarth stared at the taut-faced men. "I need hardly explain the reason for this order, but, so that it will be clear to both yourselves and the men of your commands, I will ask Dewer to reveal the psychological motivation for the order."

"One man can only control several in one of two ways," snapped the little man tersely. "He can win their trust, or he can earn their fear. I doubt that there is any question of winning the loyalty of the prisoners, and so we must instil in each man a dread and fear of authority as represented by the guards." He stared around the table. "In this respect I must point out that punishment must be immediate, public, and without hesitation. Only when the prisoners know that any hesitation or refusal in obeying an order will be punished by immediate and unalterable death, will they accept the rule of one over many."

"Thank you," said the tall Admiral and stared at the silent men. "I am having the ship go into orbit when not in use, if we left it here it would be a constant temptation to the prisoners to revolt and seize it as a means of escape." He sighed and rested his hands flat on the wide desk. "Any questions?"

They looked at each other, hesitating, each waiting for the other to speak first, and watching them, Hogarth felt a sudden irritation. Abruptly he slammed his hand down on the desk and the sharp sound echoed heavily from the walls of the silent room.

"Well? Are you telling me that everything is crystal clear to you? If it is I must congratulate you on your perception, but if not, and I venture to suggest that some of you seem to have your doubts, I am willing for you to ask questions." He glowered at them. "I may not be always so willing."

"About arms, sir." One of the captains cleared his throat as the tall Admiral looked at him. "You said the object was to found a new fighting force, but what are we to arm them with, if we arm them at all that is. We have bullet guns, a few Niones, but nothing else."

"They will be armed," said Hogarth grimly, and he glanced at Rennie with secret understanding. "Anything else?"

"About the training, sir," said the other captain doubtfully. "I can understand how we must break their spirit and instil a cowering fear, but what then? How are we to replace that fear with loyalty and pride? It seems to me that as soon as we arm them they will turn the weapons against us in revenge for past treatment."

"Dewer?" Hogarth glanced at the little psychologist. "Will you answer that question for the captain."

"Yes, sir." The little man scowled at the man who'd asked the question. "A man hates what he fears and fears what he hates. But, when he becomes the thing he fears he will no longer fear it. In other words once we arm one of the prisoners he will cease to be a prisoner and become one of us, and, accepting that, he will probably be more ruthless in his attitude towards his one-time fellow prisoners than we could ever be." He yawned, not troubling to hide his impatience. "A simple problem in elementary psychology and one that has been known and understood for generations. I am surprised that you asked the question at all."

"It was a good question, Dewer," said Hogarth coldly, and something in his pale, washed out eyes made the little man shrink in his chair. "A good question and one worthy of a civil answer." He looked at the assembled men. "Any further questions? No? Then that will be all. Training schedules will be given you in ample time for you to study and understand them thoroughly." He rose and they rose with him. "That is all for now, gentlemen. Dewer, you will remain, there are one or two points on which I wish your opinion. Good night, gentlemen."

He stood, trim and neat in his grey uniform, and acknowledging their farewells with a stiff inclination of his head. Finally, they had gone, only the little psychologist remaining slumped in a chair, and the tall man thinned his lips as be resumed his seat.

"You wanted me?" Dewer asked the question with familiar ease of a man who is alone with someone he knows too well for pretence.

"Yes." Hogarth frowned down at the little man. "We have a problem, Dewer," he said slowly. "One new to me and, as far as I am aware, new to the field of which you are a member."

"A psychological problem?" The little man hunched forward. "What is it?"

Hogarth stared at the little man, a faint expression of distaste curving the corners of his mouth, and, as he stared, Dewer began to sweat and shift on his hard chair.

"You are a clever man," said Hogarth slowly. "I know that, that is why you are here instead of rotting in prison where you belong, but this time I don't want you to use your skill to turn an enemy hopelessly insane."

"It was an accident," muttered the little man. "I tried to help him, could I help it that he went off his head?"

"Perhaps, but no matter, all that is in the past." The tall man leaned forward and his pale eyes seemed to reflect the savage light of the swollen sun in redoubled splendour. "I want to do two things," he said quietly. "Two opposed things and it will take care and cunning to wed them in careful balance. I want to break a man's spirit and teach him to obey, and I want, at the same time, to strengthen his desire to survive. There you have it. Obey and survive! In that order. Obey and survive! Obey even when obedience goes against the survival instinct and to survive while obeying any possible order." He stared at the little man. "Can it be done?"

Dewer shrugged, toying with a slender pencil, his thin face furrowed in deep thought, and his mouth twisted into a down-curved line. He stared at the tall man.

"I can make a man obey," he said slowly. "Nothing simpler, but to survive?" He shrugged. "Why worry about survival value? There are always replacements."

"There were always replacements," corrected the tall Admiral grimly. "But those days are over."

He clenched one thin hand and stared down at his knuckles as they shone through waxen skin. "The Stellar Legion will be composed of men trained to the ultimate, the best fighting force ever known in the history of man. But such a force must have officers and officers must be obeyed. To operate at all the force must have a low percentage of loss, and this brings us to the problem of survival. A problem, Dewer, which you must solve."

"*Must* solve?"

"Yes. Can you do it?"

Dewer nodded and in his eyes something glowed with a feral light. He looked more devil than man, and something cold and brutal with the merciless brutality of the scientist devoted to a single aim reflected itself on his tormented features.

"I can do it," he whispered and stared at the Admiral. "A free hand?"

Hogarth nodded.

CHAPTER 6

MARCH OF TERROR

The first week was hell, sheer, unadulterated hell, and at times Wilson doubted his ability to survive. The double gravity tore at him, turning each and every muscle to a point of rasping agony, and he, together with all of the new arrivals, suffered torment from overworked ligaments and strained tendons. Then the soreness passed, his back straightened, his legs accepted and compensated for the extra burden of a too-heavy body, and he was ready for the second stage of his training.

It consisted entirely of calisthenics and elaborate exercises designed to build muscle and tone up the system. The food was better than any he had ever known, rich and nourishing, filling his shrunken stomach and covering his bones with fat and firm flesh. Regularly they all had assorted injections, injections that hurt and made him feel sick for several hours, his body burning with a strange feverishness as his system absorbed the varied drugs and stimulants, the gland extracts and hormones prescribed by the doctor.

Some men died. Some men went into raving insanity as their drugged bodies craved for unobtainable narcotics and liquid poisons. They twisted on their narrow bunks, making the sleep periods hideous with their continual moaning and frenzied pleadings for that which they could not have.

They vanished those men, disappearing into some great unknown, and none mourned their passing. Sleep period followed sleep period, and they worked at various apparatus, lifting great weights, running, jumping, standing tensed and strained as they supported heavy masses, climbing rough walls, marching, skipping, a continual never-ending monotony of physical effort.

At the end of a month they gathered in the cleared area before the Admin buildings forty-five now instead of the original fifty, and many of them seemed on the point of collapse, their hearts weakened by age and overstrain, their systems ruined by trying to do too much too soon.

Wilson stared curiously at the trim uniformed figure of the tall Admiral and listened, half-attentively, to the heavy words echoing flatly around.

"You have now passed your first period of training and are as fit as four weeks of concentrated effort can make you. Some of you are weak, some strong, some indifferent, others interested, and all of you are probably wondering what is going to happen to you. I shall not enlighten you. You will do as ordered, merely that and nothing else, and, as long as you obey, you will have nothing to fear. That is all."

The tall figure turned, answered the salute of a short, stocky captain, and strode towards the Admin building. Next to Wilson a man spat in emphatic anger.

"The swine," he said from the corner of his mouth. "The snotty-nosed swine. I'd like to get him alone for ten minutes in some dark corner."

"Silence!" The short captain glared at the assembled men. "No talking." He glared at them, his hand resting on the holstered weapon at his waist, and Wilson felt a sudden fear. Up to now everything had gone at such a speed that he'd had little time for thought. He had worked hard and slept deeply, and the routine had been too near what he'd been accustomed to for him to question it too closely, but now, staring at the sweating face of the stocky captain, he was reminded forcibly of the overseer and what he had suffered at the dead man's hands.

The officer was dangerous.

Next to him the man fell silent and a hush fell over the clustered men. They stood, sweating beneath the swollen sun, and beneath their feet the sand felt hot and gritty.

"We're going for a walk," snapped the captain with grim humour. "A nice long walk over the desert and we're not stopping for anything, not for food, for water, for rest, or for death." He grinned at them, a tight, humourless twisting of his mouth. "I'm going to tell you once and once only. We're not going to stop for anything.

So, if you fall out, you've had it. If you want to live you'll keep moving."

He gestured to a small group of uniformed guards and they walked towards him, sub-guns cradled in their arms and canteens hanging over their shoulders.

"Attention! Left turn! Quick…march!"

Smartly they strode over the desert, walking in strict rhythm towards the fiery ball of the swollen sun, and behind them, sheltered behind high windows, Hogarth watched them go. Beside him the little psychologist tittered with nervous laughter and rubbed his thin, claw-like hands together in secret amusement.

The first hour wasn't too bad. In a way it was a relief to stretch their legs in a steady, monotonous, strictly mechanical time. Wilson was almost glad of the opportunity to think, to let his legs carry his body while his mind turned and worried at scraps of assorted information. He still felt dazed from the swift events following his killing of the overseer, the quick trial, the conviction, the long trip in a spaceship and the transfer to the penal world. Then had followed the rigorous weeks of constant effort, and now this, the seemingly pointless march into nowhere.

A second hour passed, a third, a fourth, and now thirst began to dry his throat and burn his stomach, cracking his lips and swelling his tongue. He turned his head, staring at the man beside him, and drew in his breath as he stared at the stumbling figure by his side.

The man was dying.

He dragged his feet across the sand and his broad, yellowish features were dull and tinged with grey. His eyes were half closed, looking like twin slits and his cracked lips were puffed and framed a swollen, leatherish tongue. Startled, Wilson stared at the other men, twisting his head and looking behind him, shocked at what he saw.

Some, like himself, seemed unaffected. Others, like the man at his side, appeared to be at the last gasp, the rest were halfway between and one man, a tall, thin, white-haired man with the face of a ravaged saint, appeared to be praying, praying or mouthing a stream of curses as he stared up at the brassy bowl of the sky.

Still they marched towards the swollen sun.

Two hours later, the first man fell out. He dropped like a sack of mush, his legs and arms sprawling over the hot sand, his mouth open, and his eyes glazed and dull. Instinctively the column slowed and the short captain snarled at them with savage anger.

"Keep in step you scum! Keep moving!"

"Wait!" The tall man with the saintly features stepped out of line and knelt beside the fallen man. "We can't leave him here."

"Get back in line and keep moving!" The captain glared down at the tall man, his lips drawn tight against his teeth, his hand gripping the butt of his pistol. The tall man shook his head.

"No. I…"

The sound of the shot echoed flatly over the desert, coinciding with a rush of red leaping from the white hair, turning it into a soggy mess.

"You heard what I said," roared the officer. "Move!"

He stared at them, the pistol a glinting finger of menace in his hand, his eyes glittering from the shadow of his visored cap. He ignored the body a his feet.

They moved. They resumed the march with leaden feet and a cold something twisting at their stomachs, and behind them, dark against the ochre and, two bodies lay, supine and lifeless, dwindling into black specks as they fell far behind.

And now fear and terror marched with them into the furnace fury of the searing desert.

To fall out was to be left behind to die. To help a comrade was to die, and, for the first time, Wilson realised just what he was up against, what all the prisoners were up against. The guards weren't joking, the Admiral hadn't just been making a noise, the tall man with the once white hair had proved that, he had been shot down because he hesitated at obeying an order, shot down like a dog.

And it could happen to any of them.

Slowly the hours passed. Slowly they swung in a wide arc and now the glaring sun struck at their backs instead of their faces and they knew that they were on their way back to the settlement. Thirst clawed at them like a ravening thing, a thirst increased by the sight of the guards drinking from their canteens and splashing water over their heads. The guards drank, but the men did not drink, and they stumbled over the gritty sand, each man lost in his own private hell.

The grey-faced man next to Wilson stumbled and fell, a man cursed as he tripped over the limp figure; and another swore as he lost step. No one stopped, no one halted to aid the fallen man, they had learned their lesson.

Another fell, another, their piteous cries following the marching men, pleading for help, for water, for a brief rest. They were ignored, and, cowed by the menacing guns of the guards and hardened by their own misery, the prisoners stumbled on with deaf ears and iron faces.

Twelve hours after they had left they returned to the settlement, forty of the original forty-five, and like things of wood, without sense or feeling, they flung themselves at a wide trough filled with cold water. They drank, they gulped at the sweet fluid, rolling in it, laving their faces and hands, gulping and gulping in a desperate effort to replace their lost moisture.

The guards looked on with cynical eyes.

Sense came almost too late. Wilson recoiled from the water and dragged at the shoulder of a man at his side.

"Take it easy. You can kill yourself like that."

"What?" The man, a slim, shrewd-eyed, yellow-skinned native of the Sirian System, jerked at the restraining arm. "Let me alone, damn you. I'm thirsty."

"Maybe, but if you drink too deep you'll get colic and that can be fatal." The young man stared at the watching guards. "Look at them, they know what can happen."

"Yeah." The yellow-faced man wiped his lips with a thoughtful gesture. "You're right. Thanks." He jerked other men away from the trough, heedless of their cursing, and both he and Wilson tried to get some semblance of reason into the thirst-crazed men. Some listened to reason, some, either from past experience or from ingrained caution, had already moved from the water, others, animal-like in their blind obeying of instinct, slobbered and fought their way back to the sweet water.

Later, when they had been locked in for the sleep period, and their rations had been eaten, Wilson learned the entire reason for the apparently pointless march.

He learned the hard way, writhing on his bunk from the pain in his stomach and around him moaning and crying, the men who had drunk too deeply too soon, rolled and cursed with inner anguish. Some screamed, some snarled, some died, but they all learned.

The yellow-skinned native of the Sirian System groaned as he pressed his hands to his swollen stomach, and stared at the young man with bitter eyes.

"The swine," he gritted. "The dirty stinking swine. They didn't have to do this to us, did they?"

"No," agreed the young man, "but they did." He frowned. "I wonder why?"

"Maybe they want to kill us?" The man groaned. "I don't know why they did it, but something tells me a man could use a friend, lots of friends." He wiped sweat from his sere features. "My name's Conroy."

"Wilson." The young man winced at the screams from a dying man. "If you look at it one way," he said slowly, "the whole thing makes sense. They train us and then march us out into the desert. The weak fall out, those who try to help the fallen get killed, then, after a long time, when we're all half crazy with thirst, they bring us back and let us drink. They could have stopped us or rationed the water, but no, they just left us on our own."

"Why?"

"To teach us a lesson," said Wilson grimly. "A simple thing really and they did it the hard way. It is dangerous to drink too deeply after a long hot march." He stared grimly at the taut face of his new friend. "I don't think that any of us will ever forget that lesson, those that live through it anyway."

"A lesson?" Conroy thinned his lips. "A hell of a way to teach a lesson. But why, Wilson? Why?"

"I don't know, but you remember what the Admiral said? He promised that half of us would be dead within four months, and that if ten of us were alive at the end of a year he would be satisfied. I didn't pay much attention at the time, none of us did, but now I'm beginning to realise what he meant."

"What?"

"They're weeding us out. The weak, the stubborn, the ones who are slow to obey. They die, one way or another they die, and only the best, the hardest, the most cowed are left."

"You could be right," agreed Conroy, and gently rubbed his sore stomach. "I wish that they left me in jail," he snarled. "This is worse than the gas chamber, at least that death would have been quick and neat, but this…" He spat.

"You think that they are going to kill us all?"

"Why not? This is a penal world isn't it?" Conroy shrugged. "I thought that they'd put us to forced labour, farming, mining, something like that. But it seems that I was wrong. That crazy Admiral must have ideas of his own." He frowned thoughtfully at the low roof. "I wonder what his idea is?"

"To break our spirit and to weed us out." Wilson rolled on his hard bunk, trying to ease sore muscles and aching bones, and tried not to listen to the groans of the dying. "I don't think that the idea is to kill us all. I've been thinking and I've noticed that there doesn't seem to be many guards. Maybe they want to use us as guards for the new arrivals."

"I hope that they do," said Conroy grimly. "If they do they'll have to arm us, and then…" He chuckled, a thick sound of raw anticipation. "Man! Will they get a surprise!"

"Yes," said the young man, and frowned. "It doesn't seem to make sense," he admitted. "If they arm us they'll be asking for trouble, but unless they arm us we can't act as guards." He stretched. "Anyway, the worst seems to be over."

"What makes you think that?"

"It's obvious. We've lost ten men already, and maybe more will have died by this morning. They can't want to kill us all, if they did, then they'd do it and get it over with."

"Then there'll be no more marches?" Conroy settled himself for sleep. "I hope you're right."

"I'm right," said Wilson with quiet conviction.

He was wrong.

CHAPTER 7

KILL OR BE KILLED

They marched the next day, and the next, and the day after that. Long, seemingly pointless marches, the remaining thirty-seven men of the original batch, the tough and the fit, the ones who had recovered from the strain of early training and who had taken care when they drank. They marched towards the nightside and shivered with bitter cold, towards the dayside and sweated with searing heat. They had water on these marches, and food, and each man was loaded with his own weight of sand, the heavy packs cutting into tender flesh.

They slept deeply and ate voraciously and the clear glow of health suffused their skins and cleared their eyes. Muscles bulged where none had bulged before, bones stiffened beneath the action of the regular injections, and men who had been weedy and thin grew and developed into what men should be.

Together with the training came a sense of comradeship, the inevitable reaction of men who lived and worked together, who suffered the same pains and shared the same hardships, and, as that comradeship grew, the guards became uneasy.

They were too few, and they knew it. Five men to control fifty, and despite their ready guns and the constant threat of death, the prisoners looked at them, and waited, and naked murder shone in their narrowed eyes.

A week passed and the marches stopped. Now they dug trenches, long shallow pits, labouring with heavy shovels beneath the double gravity. A few fell out, a few hesitated at a snapped command and died with bullet-smashed skulls, the rest nursed their hate and bided their time. Thirty now out of fifty, and Wilson remembered the grim promise of the tall Admiral.

He wondered how the rest would die.

His friendship with the yellow-skinned man had grown and he and Conroy talked for long hours during the brief periods when, locked in their quarters, they rested before sleep.

"You know," said the Sirian one 'night', "I've been thinking. All this training, the marching, the digging, you know what it reminds me of?"

"What?"

"An army, that's what. I used to read a bit when young and some of the books were about the old wars and the ancient land forces they had then. Those men used to do all this, toning themselves up and practising actual combat conditions." He spat thoughtfully at a drift of sand. "No one does it now, of course, there's no sense in it. Wars are fought with machines and space ships, atomic bombs and energy weapons, but I wouldn't be surprised to learn that the old man had some weird idea of turning us into an army."

"How could he do that?" Wilson twisted on his narrow bunk and stared at his friend. "That means he intends to arm us, and the day he does…"

"Yeah." Conroy licked his lips. "He must be a fool. The way things are going we're all ready to gang up and jump the guards. Once we get our hands on some guns they won't stand a chance."

"We've lost a lot of men," reminded the young man. "Most of them shot for refusing to obey. You think that the rest will take a chance like that?"

"Why not?" Conroy echoed his surprise. "Our batch has lost more men than any other, but we had a lot of weaklings to start with." He stared at Wilson. "I've been watching the others, did you know that there are almost three hundred men here now? Prisoners I mean, toughened men, those who have managed to live this long. I doubt if then are more than fifty guards and they can't keep us under for ever. In a little while, when we get more men sent here, the lid will blow off and we'll take over." He licked his lips in savage anticipation.

"I've got plans for some of them, personal plans. The captain, Rennie I think his name is, I'm going to cut his eyelids off and rub sand in the wounds. Then I'm going to cut off his hands and feet and make him walk into the desert. The swine! I've seen him kill five men in cold blood."

Wilson didn't reply. Like most of the prisoners he hated the guards, but he couldn't relish the thought of torture and maiming a man, even though the man was an enemy. If death had to come it should be quick and clean and merciless, not the sadistic gloating over riven flesh and screaming pain desired by things who were more animal than man.

He turned on his side, half-disgusted with Conroy for thinking about such things, and yet, within himself, a tiny spot of his own secret nature relished the idea of turning the tables, of swift and violent action, and the resulting freedom from living in constant fear of a smashing bullet, of having to answer to the hard-faced men in grey and scarlet, of torturing himself for no obvious reason.

The next day there was a change.

They returned from an arduous day's work to find their bunks occupied by tense-faced men from another batch. They glared at each other, the new arrivals and the original occupants, and Conroy snarled an oath.

"Out of there, you! I'm tired."

"Go to hell," said a big man curtly, and stretched on the narrow bunk. "They shifted us in here and this is where we belong."

"Wait!" Wilson stepped forward and caught the yellow-skinned man by the arm. "Maybe there's been a mistake."

"What if there has? I'm tired and I want to get some rest." He glared at the man occupying his bunk. "Out!"

"Yeah?" The man grinned. "Suppose you make me?"

"Hold it," snapped Wilson. "I'm going to see the guard. Someone's slipped up somewhere." He glanced at the crowded room. "There's twice as many men here as there are bunks. Surely they don't expect us to sleep on the floor?"

"I'm sleeping on no floor," said Conroy grimly. "I don't care who flops down on the dirt but it's not going to be me."

Wilson shrugged and, going to the locked panel, hammered on the metal door. After several minutes a guard swung back the Judas window and glared at him.

"Well?"

"There's been a mistake," said the young man quickly. "We've too many men in here."

"There's been no mistake," snapped the guard. "Are you arguing with me?" Metal gleamed from the slender barrel of a pistol and Wilson swallowed as he shook his head.

"No, sir. But what happens to the men without a bunk to sleep on?"

"What's the matter with the floor?" The guard laughed at the young man's expression and slammed the panel. Conroy glowered at him when he returned.

"Well?"

"There's been no mistake," said Wilson dully. "Some of us will have to bunk on the floor."

"Not me," snapped the yellow-skinned man. "I'm tired." He glared at the big man on his bunk. "Right. Do you get out peaceful, or do I drag you out?"

"Like hell!"

"Okay, fellow," snapped Conroy. "You asked for it."

The big man met his lunge with a smashing blow to the face and Conroy staggered back, blood gushing from his broken nose. He crouched, snarling, then turned and grabbed at another occupant of a bunk. He tugged and the man, a slight, rat-like fellow, swore as he crashed to the floor.

"You dirty swine! I'll…"

"You'll what?" Conroy spat at him and deliberately climbed into the bunk. "If you want to sleep easy go and find yourself another bed. This one's mine." He laughed as the rat-like man scurried towards another sleeping place. He winked at the young man.

"Grab yourself a bunk, Wilson. Be tough or you'll have sore bones. Jerk some drip out and climb in."

Wilson hesitated, glancing to where men swore and struggled as they fought over who was to sleep on the hard cots. He shrugged, and, finding a corner of the room, settled himself on the rough surface and tried to sleep. It was a long time coming, and when he awoke, he ached from toes to the top of his skull.

He slept on the floor for three periods, then, deep within him, something revolted.

They had worked hard that day and he was tired and sick, aching from his rough bed and angry at those who refused to alternate the relative comfort of the bunks so that others could have a turn.

He crossed the room to where a man sat on the edge of what had been his bunk.

"Don't you think that it's about time I had a go at sleeping easy?"

The man stared at him, noting the obvious youth and lack of experience of the man, the smooth tone of his voice and his apparent desire to avoid combat.

He spat.

It was as if he threw a switch, released a trigger on pent-up emotions, freeing all the frustration and anger, the bottled up hate and fury boiling unsuspected, deep within the young man. Wilson trembled, feeling the twin emotions of hate and fear churn in his stomach, and, as he had done once before, lost himself completely to savage anger.

Blood spurted beneath his clenched fist and cartilage crumbled to a messy pulp. He struck again, desperate with the knowledge that, if he gave the man a second's opportunity, he would suffer for it. A foot lashed at his groin and he twisted, his thigh numbing from the force of the blow. Snarling, the man, his face a mask of blood from his crushed nose, advanced to the attack.

He was big, well-muscled, and with the one great advantage of having an animal nature tested and hardened by experience. He had killed before and he was willing to kill again.

Wilson staggered as a heavy fists slammed against his body. A knee thrust at him and he doubled in retching agony, a fist thudded against his mouth and he reeled, spitting blood and fighting for breath. Dimly he saw the blood-streaked features of the big man advance towards him and calmly and dimly, as if from far away, he heard Conroy's voice.

"His eyes, boy. Blind him! Stab at his eyes!"

He ducked and felt air stir his cheek as the savage blow missed. He twisted, his fists slamming at the big man's face, slamming with all the force of young muscles trained beneath double gravity. Feet lashed at him, heavy feet, still booted and aimed at his stomach and groin. He sprang aside, gripped a foot, and twisted with frantic energy.

The big man screamed, twisting as ligaments tore in his hip, throwing himself frantically in the same direction as his rotated foot in an effort to prevent broken bones and dislocated joints. He fell, his forehead smashing against the floor, and suddenly the fight was over.

Wilson gasped, wiping blood from his face, and staggered towards the bunk. A hand gripped his shoulder, twisting him away, and a man leered at him as he slipped between Wilson and the bunk.

"This is mine, buster. Thanks for getting it for me—"

He shrieked, doubling, his eyes starting from his head, and sweat oozing from his pockmarked features as he grovelled on the floor, and Wilson stared down at him, feeling a numbness in his knee, and slowly realising that his automatic reaction had dictated the abrupt, unthinking blow.

Tiredly he stretched himself on the bunk.

"Good for you, boy," chuckled Conroy. "I liked the way you used the knee on that character, but you'll have to watch yourself in future, you almost went under with the big guy."

"Did I?" Wilson slumped with the shock of exhaustion and wished the yellow-faced man would stop talking.

"Yeah. You had the right idea, smash 'em before they know it's coming, but you were too gentle with him." Conroy spat on the limp figure of the unconscious man. "You should have stabbed at his eyes, blinded him, then given him the boot." He stared seriously at the young man. "Remember this, Wilson, never give anyone a chance. Never. If you're going to hurt them, then do it quick and do it good. Don't play with them, and don't give them a chance of hurting you. Smash 'em, give them all you've got, and make sure, very sure, that they can't hurt you back."

"Kill them you mean?"

"What else?"

Wilson shuddered, admitting the cold logic of what the other man said, and yet not liking to hear it. He hated the thought of violence, he had seen too much of it all during his formative years, and he had always been on the receiving end. Conroy must have sensed his distaste for he leaned forward and when he spoke his voice was very serious.

"Look, Wilson, I like you, and I'd do a lot for you, but there are some things you've got to learn. This is a tough life and you've got to be tougher than it is if you're going to survive. No one will give you anything, no one will help you, no one gives a single damn about you. You know that. If you didn't you wouldn't be here at all, but you've killed a man, maybe more than one, and it's no good shutting your eyes to the fact."

He grunted as the big man staggered to his feet and stumbled away to a corner.

"You see? You could have stayed on the floor but you have guts enough to fight for what you wanted. That's the way it is and that's the way it's going to be. You've got to be hard and ruthless, hit first and hit hard, kill if you have to but cringe to no man. Trust no one, confide in no one, make yourself self-sufficient and to hell with the rest." He chuckled, half-ashamed of his own intensity, and yet wholly sincere. Wilson knew that he was listening to a personal philosophy of man-made jungles and man-made outlaws, and, even though he did not believe in what the yellow-faced man said, yet he admitted the truth of his words.

Kill or be killed!

Eat or be eaten, the old, tried and tested law of the jungle, cruel, merciless, and yet a law which had worked and still worked whenever men congregated despite all the idealists and peace-preachers to the contrary.

Number one first, last, and all the time, and to hell with the rest.

A good credo, a very good credo—when surrounded by convicted killers and the scum of a galaxy, ruled by trigger-happy guards, and worked and trained in a living hell. A creed that could save a man's life, save his reason, enable him to live where others would die, let him ignore pain and suffering, the weak and helpless, the pleas and prayers of those who still clung to useless ideals.

A very good creed indeed.

CHAPTER 8

DIVIDE AND RULE

Captain Rennie stood, wide legged beneath the blazing sun, and felt his nerves jump and crawl over his soggy skin. Before him a group of men stood in long lines, facing each other, each with a long pole in their hands. They were stripped to the waist and on their tanned skins great weals and bruises showed against the smooth flesh.

"Right," he snapped, and the butt of his pistol felt heavy in his hand. "Try again. Attack!"

Immediately the men began to lash at each other with the long, heavy poles. They fought with a rim, savage violence, and the smack of wood on flesh and bone echoed flatly through the thick air. Rennie watched them with sick disgust.

Scum, he thought, unwanted scum, and it was his job to turn them into soldiers. They had received full hypno-tuition on un-armed combat, learning all the tricks of judo and jungle fighting, learned the weak points and the nerve centres, and now they were putting their knowledge to practice. The heavy poles, harmful as they were, yet enabled a man to receive several blows without any real danger, and with them the men learned coordination and reflex action.

But they were as dangerous as cornered rats.

An old man passed near to him, a dry and sere old man, useless for anything but routine fatigue duties, a misfit working out what remained of his life cleaning latrines and preparing food. Rennie called to him.

"You, there!"

"Yes, sir?"

"Clean my boots." Immediately, without the slightest hesitation, the man knelt and rubbed dust from the high leather knee boots.

Rennie glowered down at him, then, with sudden contempt, thrust him sprawling in the dust.

"Get out of here! Fast!"

"Yes, sir. At once, sir." Painfully the old man limped away, and Rennie became aware of a sudden hush.

The men had stopped fighting.

They stared at him, the hard poles tight in their hands, and fear clawed at the stocky captain at the expression he read in their eyes.

"Attack!" he snarled. "Now!"

For a moment he thought that they would hesitate, and sunlight glanced from the machine pistol in his hand. He levelled the weapon, his finger tightening around the trigger, then the heavy air resounded to the smack of wood on wood and wood on flesh. Rennie grinned. Scum, but they recognised their masters.

He watched them for a while, judging with a shrewd eye the state of their physical exhaustion, then rapped a curt order. The men broke apart, resting their crude weapons on the sand, their chests heaving as they sucked great breaths of the thick air.

Deliberately he walked between the long lines.

Hate welled around him, the frustrated, savage hate of men driven almost to the breaking point but held back by the fear of certain death. Rennie grinned, drawing his lips hard against his teeth, feeling his nerves crawl with anticipation, and yet relishing his mastery over these trained animals. He paused, staring at a young man, a man scarcely more than a boy, with the blue scars of radiation burns mottling the left side of his neck and cheek.

"You, there! Clean my boots."

"Yes, sir." Wilson knelt and brushed the dust from the captain's glistening boots. He kept his head lowered to hide the expression in his eyes. Rennie sneered as he stared down at the curved back of the man at his feet.

"That's enough." He stared around him, "You there! Eat sand!"

"What?"

"You heard me! Eat sand."

"Yes, sir." Obediently the man scooped up a handful of the gritty soil and thrust it into his mouth. Rennie nodded and walked away, swaggering a little, knowing that the men behind him longed to rend and tear his quivering flesh, longed, but dared not.

He was still the master.

But for how long?

It was cool inside the Admin building, cool and fresh after the heat of outside, and Rennie paused to wipe his face and neck, then, hitching his weapon belt higher around his waist and brushing his grey uniform, he entered the conference room.

Hogarth nodded towards him, gesturing for him to take a seat, and Rennie grunted as he slumped into a chair between the doctor and the little psychologist. The tall Admiral cleared his throat.

"Report on progress. Rennie?"

"The men are as well trained in a physical sense as we can expect in the short time and limited facilities at our disposal," said the stocky captain. "Discipline is good but is nearing the breaking point. I wouldn't like to predict how long we can last without an outbreak of mutiny, but it can't be long."

"Dewer?"

"The captain is correct in what he says. The men have been subjected to intense emotional and physical strain. Their spirits are not yet broken, however, and they will not break until they have tried and failed to kill the guards and take over the settlement."

"That we can't allow," snapped Rennie. "The guards are overworked as it is and a mutiny can only result in heavy losses to both sides."

"Please!" Hogarth stared coldly at the captain. "Doctor?"

"No disease, general health excellent, the weak have died." The doctor rapped his report with the abrupt explosion of a machine gun. Hogarth nodded.

"Good. We have been on Stellar for almost four months now and of the original intake of four hundred men two hundred and fifty have survived, and are fit for the next stage. We have twenty camp orderlies, old men who obviously weren't worth the effort of attempting to train, those men can be replaced at the next intake."

"When will that be, sir?"

"As soon as we can augment the guards, Rennie, I have asked for them to be transhipped awaiting our orders." He stared at the short captain. "As soon as we can finish the basic training of the men we have we will send for them."

"Yes, sir. But what about the mutiny?"

"Dewer?" Hogarth glanced at the little psychologist and Dewer cleared his throat.

"There will be no mutiny," he said sharply. "I have kept close watch on the emotional index of the prisoners and we will act long before they can be ready." He glanced at the impassive features of the tall Admiral. "As yet we have concentrated on their physical well-being and the instilling of complete obedience. We have also taken the opportunity of teaching one or two basic lessons in military requirements, but they have been minor and were incidental to the main purpose. I refer of course to the forced marches and the temptation of liberal water, the confining of too many men in quarters which only held beds for half that number, and the practice of issuing food and water in bulk rations so that the strong obtained more than the weak. There has been some fighting, but nothing serious. I doubt if more than ten men lost their lives and not more than fifteen were seriously wounded. However, the practice served its purpose of delaying close cohesion between the men and the fermenting of individual antagonism." He gave a dry chuckle. "The old principle of divide and rule."

"Divide and rule?" Rennie frowned. "I don't get it."

"He means that while the men are busy fighting among themselves we've got nothing to worry about," explained the doctor. He glanced at the little man, "But they solved that problem didn't they?"

"Yes," admitted Dewer. "They did. Several strong men arose and forced a system of rationing and bed rotation." He shrugged. "Surprising considering what they are, but not entirely unexpected."

"But what about the threatened mutiny?" insisted Rennie curtly. "I don't like it. I've seen such things before and, guns or not, we wouldn't stand a chance against them if they rose against us."

"They won't rise," said Dewer drily. Rennie flushed.

"That's what you say, but you don't have to go out there, I do. I can feel it, feel the hate and fear, and, as soon as the hate gets a little stronger, we've had it."

"That will do, Rennie!" Hogarth's voice slashed across the room. "I am responsible for the running of this settlement."

"Yes, sir, but..."

"No arguments, Rennie!" The tall Admiral glared at the stocky officer. "Things are under full control. Dewer?"

"Yes, sir."

"Explain."

"As you wish, sir." The little man sneered at the captain. "Very well then, in words of one syllable, we are ready to carry out the next stage of the programme."

"Which is?"

"Destroying the cohesion between the men." Dewer chuckled as he saw the blank expression on the captain's face. "Really, Rennie, you should leave these matters to those who understand them."

"I asked you to explain," snapped the Admiral coldly. "Please do so without further delay."

"Yes, sir." Twin spots of red showed for a moment on the little man's sallow cheeks. "The one danger we face is that the men will group together and act in concert. In normal armies this danger is remote, the men are amenable to discipline, and have the weight of tradition to keep them in order Even so, however, mutinies have been known, and our problem is a little more pressing than normal. We are dealing with scum, killers, men who have murdered and who, logically, would have no compunction at murdering again. It is essential that we forestall any attempts at concerted action."

"I know that," grumbled Rennie. "But how?"

"We will make them hate each other more than they hate us." Dewer paused, and in the following silence the sounds of men at drill echoed faintly in the room.

"Very nice," sneered the captain. "Now tell me how to perform this miracle."

"Reward and punishment." Dewer leaned back in his chair. "The men have no real affinity to each other. They are all lone wolves, misfits, unwanted and unwanting. Very well, then. We set one against the other with promotion as the reward to the winner. Naturally, at first, we shall arm the winners with staves and clubs. Later, when we are sure of them, we can issue weapons, and, by so doing, found a circle of men into guards, guards into officers, and each rank will be earned and by so earning, the winner will feel nothing but contempt for the loser." He shrugged. "The inevitable result must be mutual hate between the men. Hate from the under-dog, for nothing is so bad as a one-time friend being elevated and using his new authority, and contempt from the winner at those less able to climb to high rank."

"Wait!" The doctor leaned forward, his eyes glistening with interest. "A suggestion. What if we make it so that a first rank officer can lose it to any man who can best him? In other words if a man can take a rank, then it's his to hold for as long as possible."

"That can come later," snapped the little psychologist impatiently. "At the moment the problem is to both break the impending mutiny and weed out men."

"Weed them out?" Rennie echoed his surprise. "That has been done already."

"No." It was the tall Admiral who spoke and his voice held a cold decision. "We have trained a group of physically fit animals, but I want more than that, I want men. I want men who have the intelligence to survive no matter at what cost. I want men who can weigh an opportunity, value a chance, solve a problem and strike when the need arises. Men who will obey, but men who can think. Not animals. Not scum. But men, the best men possible from the material we have."

"And you shall have them!" Dewer leaned across the wide table. "Listen, Rennie. You have two hundred and fifty men. Right?"

"Yes."

"Good. By the time we are ready for the next intake that number will have been reduced to less than half. The rest..." He chuckled. "Only the strong will survive and the strong needn't be those with the most muscle."

"So?"

"I have arranged a system of eliminating tests. You will explain, with great care, the nature of the tests to the men, but you will give no hint as to the logical answer. Understand me, Rennie, the whole thing depends on the men solving the problem for themselves." He chuckled again. "They have been well conditioned and I expect good results."

"What do I tell them?"

"Simply this. That two out of three can live. Just that, nothing more, and then you can leave the rest to them." The little man thrust forward a sheaf of papers. "Here are your orders. I suggest that you commence operations at once."

Rennie nodded, his lips tightening as he read the typed instructions, and when he looked at the psychologist his eyes held a sick horror.

Slowly he left the room.

CHAPTER 9

SURVIVAL

The march had been the worst yet, fully a hundred miles of slogging torment, and the swollen ball of Capella glared down from the heavens with an eye-searing splendour, sending ripples of heat rising from the gritty sand of the desert, sucking moisture from their bodies almost before it had time to form.

A hundred miles beneath double gravity, seventy hours of continuous advancing into the flaming jaws of hell, and at the end of it they were exhausted and on the verge of collapse.

Five columns set out from the settlement, almost the entire body of trained prisoners, and they had fanned out in different directions so that a tracked vehicle carried armed guards and supplies, and they churned ahead, dust pluming from beneath the wide tracks. They had slept little en route, eaten little and drank less, and thirst was a living torment within them.

Dully Wilson watched the vehicle slew to a halt and the stocky captain climb down onto the sand. He stood before them, his hands on his hips, and a tight smile drawing his lips hard against his teeth.

"Men," he snapped. "Listen carefully. This is in the nature of a tactical exercise and I don't intend to explain more than once. You are going to be divided into groups of three, the vehicle will transport each group well away from the others, and the trick is to get back to the settlement." He grinned. "Each group of three will be given a locator, set to the settlement, and a canteen of water. I'm afraid that we're short on water. Each canteen will hold plenty for one, maybe enough for two, but not enough for three. You are a hundred miles from home and comfort, water and food. I don't care how you get back, but if you don't, then it's lights out."

He turned to the vehicle.

"Right. The quicker we get started the sooner we'll all be home. One other thing. Those who return will receive first rank promotion, that means plenty of food, plenty of rest, and the job of bossing the new intake. Now. Line up and get your gear."

It was soon done. One after the other groups of three were expelled from the vehicle and stood, half-dazed, on the burning sand. Wilson had Conroy and another man as partners, Conroy holding the water and the other man the locating device. Grimly they began to plod towards the distant settlement.

It wasn't until then that the diabolical ingenuity of the whole thing struck the young man.

They had water, but not enough for the three of them. They had a locator device that made it certain they would get back to the settlement—but not enough water. Two of them had a chance. Two out of three. The third?

Wilson tried not to think about it.

Conroy was the one who put it into words. He trudged alongside Wilson, the canteen slung over one shoulder and spoke, prisonwise, from the corner of his mouth.

"What about it, Wilson?"

"What about what?"

"The third man." Conroy jerked his head towards the other member of the group. "This water won't last the three of us, I could drink it all myself, and trouble's coming unless we move first."

"He's got the locator," reminded the young man.

"I know it." Conroy chuckled. "He won't have it for long." He looked at the young man. "A bit of luck us being together. I wonder how the rest are getting on? It's nice to have someone I can trust on a job like this."

"How do you mean?"

"Are you that dumb?" Conroy spat. "One of us has got to stay behind. It's not going to be me, and, if you're smart, it needn't be you." He twisted his head as the other man drew level. "What you want?"

"A drink." The man licked his lips. "God, but I'm thirsty. Let's have a swig at that canteen."

"No."

"No?" The man narrowed his eyes. "Why not? You may be carrying it but it's for us all. Give!"

Conroy ignored him and stared at Wilson.

"Okay?"

Wilson nodded and gripped the man by the elbows.

"Say! What goes on?" The man writhed in the tight grip. "Let me go." He struggled as Conroy dropped the canteen and stepped forward. Desperately he swung his heavy boot, then grunted as a rock-hard fist slammed against his jaw. He slumped, and, as he fell, Wilson slipped the locator device from his wrist and strapped it around his own. Conroy sighed and picked up the canteen.

"Let's go," he snapped. "Before this character wakes up and decides to follow us." He hesitated, staring down at the limp figure. "You go on," he said. "I'll follow."

"What are you going to do?"

"Nothing. Get moving!"

"No." Wilson stared coolly at the yellow-skinned man. "We go together, you've done enough damage for now."

"You're a fool, Wilson. Suppose he wakes up? Suppose he follows us and tries something? Let's make sure."

"Leave him alone." The young man licked cracked lips as he squinted at the swinging needle of the locator. "We'll have a drink and get moving. The longer we hang around here the worse chance we've got of making it."

Conroy grunted and unstoppered the canteen.

They walked for two hours and then slumped down to rest. Wilson stood the first watch, sitting, half-asleep, his cold grey eyes scanning the desert behind them. Once he thought he saw a distant black speck stumbling forward, but it vanished from sight and he ignored it, busy with his own thoughts. Conroy had called himself friend, they had known each other since their arrival, and they seemed to fit into each other's mood.

It had been as simple as that.

An accident that they had been together, it could have been the other way, he could have been grouped with two friends and then...

He swallowed as he visualised what would have happened. A kick, a blow, a swinging piece of rock.

A muttered word and a quick action and he would have been left to die beneath a blistering sun on an alien planet. Deep within him something seemed to harden and crystallise, something born of fear and the desperate, primeval urge to survive. He would survive! He would! And his lips thinned as he stared at the sleeping man.

Later he slept while Conroy kept watch, a brief, uneasy sleep, torn with vivid dreams in which he escaped a thousand deaths, and when he awoke he trembled and his body was drenched with the cold sweat.

Silently they continued the march.

Seventy hours it had taken them to reach the point where they had been left. Seventy hours of forced march beneath the menacing guns of the watchful guards, and they had been fresh and rested. Now...

Now each step was a torment and life was measured by the lowering of tepid water in an emptying canteen.

Wilson became acutely aware of Conroy's thoughtful gaze.

Grimly they strode towards the distant settlement, stumbling over cracked rock and treacherous fissures dragging leaden feet over the burning sand, and around them, as yet unseen, closed in other groups, men converging on a central point in little groups of three and two and one. All fighting a desperate race against time and their own weakness.

They slept again, drank, marched, slept, marched, drank, marched and marched and marched and marched, and always the swollen ball of Capella seared at their drying bodies, sinking ever so slowly towards the far horizon.

"You know," said Conroy after one sleep period. "You've altered, Wilson. You're not the man you used to be, there's a hardness in you somewhere, a tough ruthlessness." He grinned with a flash of white teeth. "I'm glad that I'm your friend."

"Are you?"

"Yes. If I wasn't I'd have to kill you." Conroy grinned again, and eased the weight of the canteen over his shoulder. "I'm beginning to see what the old man's after, and, if I'm right, there's going to be big things for the few that manage to stay alive."

"How so?"

"Isn't it obvious? They're going to need more guards. They are training the men to form an army. They're going to need officers and men at the top, and I intend being one of them." He chuckled. "Who'd have guessed it? When they sent me here I expected a life of forced labour, but now..." He chuckled again. "I can see a rich time ahead— if I can stay alive."

"Yes?" Wilson stumbled over a broken shard of heat-cracked rock. "Why didn't you kill me, Conroy?" He asked the question in a cold, almost detached voice, and the yellow-skinned man grinned.

"Why should I?"

"More water for one thing. Personal safety for another." The young man stared at his companion. "How do you know that I won't kill you?"

"Because you've too much sense." Conroy became suddenly serious. "Killing isn't a good thing, Wilson. Sometimes it's necessary, times when it is foolish not to kill, that man back there is an example. He could be stronger than we think, be following us, and one day, when we're asleep and off guard, he could creep up on us and smash our skulls. That is an avoidable risk and we should have killed him. But killing just for the sake of it?" He shook his head. "Look at it this way. We are a group of men banded together and, like it or not, we've got to stay together. Now, what would happen if a so-called tough guy went around killing anyone who looked at him?"

"What?"

"He'd die. The others would have to get rid of him in sheer self-protection. He would be anti-survival in as much as he threatened everybody, and he would have to go. So, in that, he would be destroying himself."

"I see." Wilson stared curiously at the Sirian. "You seem to know all about it."

"I do." Conroy spat. "I was a psychologist once and I can guess what's happening here. They're weeding us out, those with a strong survival instinct will win through to life and promotion, the rest...." He shrugged and kicked at the sand. "That's why I got rid of that other man when I did. If you're going to do a thing, Wilson, do it at once. The longer you wait the more chance you give the other man to beat you to it."

"I see." Wilson stared curiously at the yellow-skinned man. "Why are you telling me all this?"

"Why not?" Conroy shrugged. "I like you, and, if I can save you a few knocks, teach you the easy way, then why shouldn't I?"

He grunted, swore, and suddenly sprawled on the gritty sand. A broken rock lay by his foot and he cursed it with savage violence.

"That damn rock!" He winced as he gripped his ankle.

"Trouble?" Wilson stepped forward and gently probed at the extended foot. Conroy swore, his leg jerking in automatic reflex action.

"Steady! That hurt!"

"Can you walk?"

"I don't know." The Sirian gritted his teeth and struggled to his feet, leaning heavily on the young man. He took a step, another, then collapsed on the sand his sere features glistening with sweat and twisted with pain. "I think it's broken, Wilson. I can't stand on it."

"Let me look." Gently Wilson stripped off the heavy boot and pursed his lips as he saw the swollen ankle. He examined the joint, and beneath his hands, Conroy jerked with pain.

"Take it easy!"

"I'm being as gentle as I can." He reached for the canteen and Conroy clung to it, his eyes narrowed with suspicion. Wilson stared at him. "Give me the water."

"Why?"

"I want to bandage your foot. A damp compress, if you've only sprained it, will support the joint and enable you to walk." Impatiently he snatched the container of water and tore a strip of fabric from the tail of his blouse. Wetting it, he wrapped it tightly around the swollen ankle, ignoring the other man's grunts of pain. When he had finished, he rose, slung the canteen over his shoulder, and helped Conroy to his feet.

"Try it now."

Cautiously the yellow-skinned man rested his weight on the bandaged foot, sweating, his lips thinned with pain. Slowly he hobbled forward, leaning heavily on Wilson, and, after three steps, sagged to the desert.

"I can't do it," he groaned. "The damn bone's gone, or something. I can't walk."

"Can't you?" Wilson stared down at the helpless man, the canteen over his shoulder and his grey eyes clouded with thought. He looked at the flaring ball of the sun, glanced down at the locator strapped to his wrist, and shook the canteen. The water splashed noisily in the almost empty container.

Slowly he began to walk away.

"Wilson!"

He halted, staring at the stricken man, poised easily on the balls of his feet.

"What is it?"

"Are you going to leave me?"

"What else can I do?"

"You can't do it, not to me you can't. I'm your friend, Wilson, your friend!"

"So?"

"Look," Conroy wiped sweat from his face and neck. "We can't be far from the settlement now. You're pretty strong, you could carry me, or at least support me. It would take a little longer, but what the hell, we're not in that much of a hurry." He stared at the impassive features staring down at him. "You can't leave me like this, Wilson. Not like this. I'll die!"

"If I try and carry you, Conroy, we'll both die." Wilson sighed as he shook the canteen. "We've not been marching as fast as we should and the water isn't going to last. If you could walk it wouldn't matter, we'd still get back in time, but if I carry you it will cut our speed down too far." He stared at the helpless man. "I'm sorry, Conroy, but that's how it is."

"You're going to abandon me?" Sick horror echoed in the Sirian's voice. "Walk away and leave me to die of thirst? You can't do it, Wilson. I'll crawl, I'll drag myself along, but don't take the water, don't take the only hope I've got." He swallowed and inched himself painfully towards the tall young man. "Give me that much of a chance, damn you! Don't leave me like this!"

He dragged himself nearer and Wilson watched him, his grey eyes hard and cold with something not wholly human. Deliberately he stepped back, away from the crawling man.

"No, Conroy. You taught me too well. I'm going to live, live though everyone else dies, and you can't blame me for following your own advice." He hesitated, staring down at the crippled man, crawling like some smashed insect over the burning sand.

"Goodbye, Conroy."

He turned and walked away towards safety and water, to food and comfort, to life and promotion. Behind him, driven by a desperate will to survive the crippled man dragged himself over the desert and from his cracked lips curses streamed in an obscene tirade.

"Wilson! Give me a drink, damn you. A last drink!"

He kept walking.

"Wilson!"

He didn't turn.

"Wilson!"

Slowly the cries faded into silence, echoing and dying over the empty desert, drifting into the silence of the grave. Wilson strode on, feeling something within him wither and fade, shrivel and die, something born of the common heritage of man, soft and kind, warm and gentle, and, as it died a strange bleakness came into his grey eyes and his mouth settled into hard, cold, almost cruel lines.

He didn't look back.

CHAPTER 10

TIGER BY THE TAIL

Director Laurence pursed thick lips and frowned down at a closely typed sheaf of papers in his hand. He grunted and stared at the thin features of the old President.

"Well?"

"Have you read the report?"

"Yes."

"And your conclusions?"

The fat man shrugged. "Obviously the same as yours." He flipped the sheaf of papers with one fat finger. "Is this all we have to go on?"

"It is."

"I see." Laurance frowned at the pastel tinted wall. "I was afraid of something like this," he said quietly. "Are you certain as to the figures?"

"Unfortunately, yes." The old President sighed and leaned back in his chair. "In one year the penal world Stellar has had five thousand three hundred and twenty-five prisoners sent to it for rehabilitation. They have drawn rations sufficient for six thousand men and the quantity of drugs requisitioned has been fantastic."

"What sort of drugs?" Laurance glanced down at the report. "I've read the names but I'm no doctor, and they mean nothing to me. Dope?"

"No. Mostly hormone extracts, ultra-calcium, gland derivatives and stimulants designed to speed reflex actions." The old man shook his head. "Hogarth must be pumping his men full of chemicals."

"Yes, but why?" The fat man stirred the papers with barely concealed irritation. "What is the purpose of these drugs?"

"They increase the bone structure and reduce the syntax level. We used them towards the end of the war to enable the crews to withstand high acceleration and to step up their reactions. Hogarth must be using them for the same purpose."

"To dope the criminals?" Laurance shrugged. "It doesn't make sense. What's he trying to do?"

"Can't you guess?" The President looked directly at the fat man. "You remember his old dream, what he told us before he left for Stellar. I would say that he is building up a select force of men, doping them to withstand the double gravity, and accelerating their responses to a point far above normal."

"I think so, too," Laurance agreed. "But we knew that, and anyway, where's the harm? The prisoners were useless to us, each of them a burden to keep, feed, retain and watch. I'd say that Hogarth has done a good job. As long as he confines his activities to the penal world we have no cause for worry." He paused, conscious of the fact he was talking more to convince himself than the other man.

"Weapons?"

"Mostly bullet guns and a few Niones. The President fumbled among the papers. "Too many bullet guns and more than enough Niones. He must be using them to arm some of the prisoners, the original contingent of guards had their own weapons and would never use so many."

"Maybe he's stockpiling?"

"Yes," whispered the old man. "That's just what I'm afraid of."

For a while they sat in silence, each man busy with his own thoughts, then Laurance shrugged.

"What do his reports say?"

"The usual. High death rate due to the poor condition of the prisoners. It was because of that we began to select the men to send to Stellar, the old and weak seemed to die within a month of landing. But that isn't what worries me."

"No?"

"No." The President riffled again through his papers. "I've been checking up on war surplus and there seem to be some inaccuracies. Several ships of Hogarth's command—vanished. A great deal of stores and war material also disappeared at the same time. Normally we'd never have known about it, but I had a suspicion and set Records to checking the fate of every vessel ever built. Allowing for unexplainable mishaps and other causes, we are ten warships short, and those ships all vanished after peace was declared and ratified."

"So!" Laurance drew in his breath with a sharp hissing sound. "We have a potential dictator on our hands."

"Perhaps, but I can't believe that Hogarth would deliberately do such a thing." The old President didn't sound at all certain of what he said. "The man is loyal, we can be sure of that, but misplaced loyalty can be as dangerous as an active enemy."

"He's loyal all right," said the fat man grimly. "But to what? The Federation? Maybe, but if he is this is a peculiar way to prove it. To himself? Perhaps, but, as you say, the man is loyal. To an ideal? There I think we have it." He leaned across the wide desk. "I remember that I had a doubt when we first offered him the job of re-habilitating the criminals. I wondered just who had led whom. Now I know. Hogarth had a plan all cut and dried and like fools we gave him the best chance he could have prayed for. We gave him men and materials, an entire planet for his own use, and to make sure that we'd dug our grave deep enough, we gave him a free hand."

"I can't believe it," whispered the old man sickly. "Not Hogarth. Not the man who won the war and helped to found the Federation of Man. I can't accept it at all."

"Why not?" Laurance was deliberately curt. "Normally I would agree with you, but the man is a fanatic, the premeditation of salting away ships and supplies proves that, and such a man is dangerous. Hogarth has one ideal, the ideal that an armed force is essential to the welfare of the Federation, and he will stop at nothing to get it."

"But the man is intelligent," protested the old President. "Surely he can see that the need for armed force has passed?"

"No idealist is ever intelligent," said the fat man with quiet conviction. "On every other subject he can be wholly normal, but on his pet hobby horse he is totally insane, and, if you don't know that by now, then it's time you did." He stared at the flushed cheeks of the old man.

"Why do you think the last war was fought? Why did we struggle for a generation, blast entire cities and planets, rip and tear the established order of things? Can you answer that?"

"To bring peace and one law to all men."

"Exactly, and why? Because we are idealists. Because the Independent worlds were habited by idealists. Both sides knew that they had the only logical answer. The fact that neither side believed any other system would work resulted in the most savage conflict ever known in the entire history of man. We won, but only just, and if we had been sensible men, we would never have gone to war at all."

"You can't say that," snapped the President. "We fought, yes, but for a long term policy and the greatest good for the greatest number. If we had not gone to war the Independent worlds would have splintered into a hundred little empires, each at the other's throat. Wasn't it worth what we did to prevent that?"

"Yes," said the fat man surprisingly. "But then, I am an idealist, and so I must be right even if I have to burn a galaxy to prove it." He chuckled, breaking the mounting tension, and relaxed in his chair.

"The only point I am trying to make is that an idealist is a dangerous man. They always have been and they always will. The various creeds that tore Earth apart for centuries were promulgated and spread by them. Not because they were deliberately cruel, but because they were so convinced that they held the only answer to human happiness, that they stopped at. nothing to enforce it. The tragedy of an idealist is that he means well, but that not everyone believes in his revelations. Like De Brath fifty years ago who thought that all men could be happy if only they removed their clothes. They incarcerated him when he went around forcibly disrobing harmless people. That was amusing, matter for jest, but De Brath was a weak man with an insane idea. Hogarth isn't weak, and he is one of the most well-versed experts in military knowledge alive today. What if he decides to go around forcing others to rearm?"

"How could he?"

"You ask me that?" Laurance shook his head. "If a man breaks into your house, what do you do? Nothing? Or do you buy a gun to shoot him the next time he tries to break in? Why did merchant men in the ancient days carry cannon? And, because they carried weapons, their captured ships led directly to piracy. How was it that the Independents were so well armed? Not because of alien life, but for self-protection against their neighbours and raiding marauders. It was those weapons which made the war last so long."

"But they are all disarmed now," protested the old man. "Not even the spaceships carry guns, why should they?"

"No reason—yet." Laurance hunched his big shoulders. "But what if Hogarth starts the ball rolling? He has ships and guns and men. The first raids would be easy, the second, maybe the third, and then every ship master, every settlement, every world in the Federation would be screaming for guns to protect themselves. They'd get them, and then, when the next quarrel arose, the next argument, they go out and settle it with guns." He stared at the startled features of the President.

"Where then is your peace?"

"We have police," stammered the President. "They will keep order."

"Over all the known galaxy?" Laurance shook his head. "Impossible. You will have to increase them to the size of the Terran Fleet, for you have to protect all planets, all shipping lines, every settlement on every known world."

"We could do it."

"Could you?" The fat man leaned forward and the soft lighting made his round features bleak and old. "Where are you going to get the men?" He shrugged. "You know as well as I do that to the normal man the thought of war and military service is hateful. That is why we had to disband the Terran Fleet in the first place. And, even if we could rebuild it, how will we supply and pay for it? No, to even consider re-establishing the Fleet is to go back to where we started from. The solution lies elsewhere.

"Hogarth?"

"Yes. We may be crying at shadows, the man may be harmless, content to play with his military toys, basking in the adulation of his men, and glorying in his command over the prisoners."

"You think that?"

"No," admitted the fat man soberly. "I think that we've got hold of a tiger by the tail, a wild tiger at that." He rapped irritably on the polished surface of the wide desk. "We should have kept a closer watch."

"Perhaps we should," agreed the old President unhappily. "I did send one agent, he had ultra-wave equipment buried beneath the skin, but he didn't report. It was that which made me suspicious." He spread his hands in a helpless gesture. "We have had so much to do, Laurance, so many things to take care of. I trusted Hogarth, he was solving a pressing problem, and we had no reason to doubt his ability or motives. We still don't know that he is other than loyal and doing his best in his own way."

"No." Laurance heaved his gross bulk to his feet. "But there is one way to find out."

"Yes?"

"I'm going to Stellar. I'm going as an accredited Director of the Federation and I'm going to find out just what is in Hogarth's mind." He looked down at the old man. "I'll go in with the next intake, and I'll go unannounced." He grinned. "The trip will do me good. I can spare some of this fat, and Stellar's supposed to be a hot place."

"Yes," said the President. "So I believe." He stared up at the big man. "You'll take care, Laurance."

He wasn't smiling as he left the room.

CHAPTER II

THE STELLAR LEGION

Sergeant Wilson stood, wide-legged in the hot sun, and watched the new prisoner intake file from the great transport. He wore a neat uniform of grey, splotched with the scarlet of his insignia of rank, and a short, heavy club hung from one wrist. From the shadow of his visored cap his cold, grey eyes stared emotionlessly at the shuffling lines of new material.

Material!

That was how he thought of the assorted wrecks sent to Stellar, the pale-faced men, the shifty-eyed men, the would-be tough guys and the men who believed in smooth words and a knife in the back. Scum, the lot of them, criminal scum. Human material to be trained, knocked, kicked and bullied into shape.

Outwardly he seemed made of stone, his prematurely aged features, mottled by the old scar, set into cold, harsh lines, belying the fact that he had not yet reached maturity. Legal maturity that is, for he was far more adult than most men, and few would have believed his true age.

Inwardly he had crushed all emotion, doing what he had to do with a cold, ruthless, utterly merciless efficiency. He had killed men and watched them die, beaten men and watched them suffer, tricked them, deluded them, driven them to the very edge of insanity.

He had lived a year on Stellar.

A year of relentless, high-pressured physical and psychological training, and any man who had survived that calculated torture was more than just a man. He had been shot at, his own body serving as target during weapon training, and he had shot back, blasting the snipers with unerring aim. He had fought with knives, pitting skill against skill, defended his hard-earned rank against men eager to advance to promotion. He had risen on the bodies of many failures, for to fail was to die, and now he was within one step of becoming an inviolate officer.

But sometimes, in the lonely watches of the sleep periods, and in the twilight haze between sleep and waking, he heard again the frenzied pleading of a man who had called him friend.

A man he had left to die.

A group of prisoners marched past, slamming to an abrupt halt at a shouted order. Big men these, tough, just out of preliminary training and eager to snatch at a chance of promotion. One man, a huge giant of humanity, his muscles hardened to iron by a long sojourn in the penal mines on Jupiter, licked his lips as he glared at the trim sergeant.

Their officer, a broad-faced man with a pistol hanging at his side, nodded as he passed, then stood at a distance, a tight smile on his lips. Wilson sighed, knowing what was coming, knowing too that the process of pitting man against man, stirring hatred and jealousy, the weeding out by sheer survival value, never ceased until a man earned the coveted rank of officer.

Imperceptibly he tensed his muscles.

"You, there," snapped the big man. "You with the stripes."

"Well?"

"I want your rank, buster. They tell me that if I can take it, it's mine. Right?"

"You can try," said Wilson coldly. "You won't get my rank, but you'll be promoted if you win."

"Yeah?" The big man grinned. "Now ain't that dandy." He knotted huge muscles. "Seems a pity to kill a kid, but what the hell?" His slit eyes flickered to the watching officer, and Wilson knew that the whole thing had been planned.

Almost he felt sorry for the giant.

He avoided the first rush merely by stepping aside, his speeded reflexes making the huge man seem slow. Slow, but not that slow, for he too had been treated with drugs and he had the advantage of being used to a three times normal gravity. At the second rush the big man snatched for the club, the only advantage a promoted man had over the rank and file. He grabbed, missed, and Wilson swung into action.

Deliberately he kicked the big man on the knee, swaying slightly as he avoided the reaching hands. The man yelled, swore, and hopped as he nursed the broken joint. Then, because men were watching, because he had to set an example to the new arrivals, and because it was criminal folly to leave an enemy able to nurse hate and plan revenge, he killed the big man.

Sombrely he stared down at the limp corpse, then looked up as a man touched his arm.

"Well?"

"My name's Laurance." the big man wiped his glistening features and nodded towards the dead man. "Did you have to do that?"

"Do what?"

"Break his neck."

"Who are you to ask questions?" Wilson didn't raise his voice but something in his eyes made the fat man recoil.

"I'm not a prisoner," he said hastily. "I am an accredited Director of the Federation." He stared at the limp body. "Why did you do it?"

"He attacked me."

"I know, I saw it, but why kill him? You had him so that he couldn't hurt you, why didn't you leave it at that?" He stared curiously at the young, strangely old man in grey. "Won't you be punished for it?"

"No," snapped Wilson curtly. Privately he thought the fat man something of a fool. Surely it was obvious that he'd had to kill the man. Survival depended on the elimination of enemies, and charity was something only the dead believed in. He turned, saluting smartly as an officer approached, and stood to rigid attention.

"At ease," snapped Rennie. He stared at the fat man. "Are you, Laurance?"

"Yes."

"Admiral Hogarth is waiting for you." He nodded to Wilson. "Continue with your duties, sergeant. I will take care of our visitor."

He led the way towards the coolness of the Admin building.

Hogarth smiled at the fat man as he wheezed his way into the coolness of the inner room and dismissed Rennie with a sharp gesture of his patrician head. Casually he waved Laurance to a seat, then leaned back, his pale, washed out blue eyes wary.

"This is an unexpected pleasure," he said carefully. "You should have notified me that you were coming."

"So that you could have cleaned up?"

"I don't understand you."

"Don't you?" The fat man stared at the blank features of the tall man. "Skip it," he said wearily. "I didn't come here to argue with you over trifles."

"No?" Hogarth parted his thin lips in the shape of a smile. "Then why did you come?"

"To find out just what's back of all this." Laurance gestured towards the high windows. "Frankly, Hogarth, you've got us worried, and I don't mind admitting it."

"Worried?" The thin smile grew broader. "What about?"

"This private army you seem to be raising here. The guns and other stores, too many guns for normal requirements, and far too many for a handful of guards." He stared at the smiling figure. "And that's another thing. You've never requested more guards, not since the day you landed, and you've been sent more than five thousand prisoners."

"Should I have done?"

"Certainly. How can fifty guards control five thousand desperate men?"

"Fifteen hundred men, Laurance," corrected Hogarth quietly. "And they control themselves."

"What!" Laurance straightened in his chair and glared at the Admiral. "Fifteen hundred? But you've had more than five thousand in the past year. Where are they?"

"Dead."

"Dead?"

"Yes, Laurance, dead. Are you surprised?" Hogarth seemed to be enjoying a secret amusement as he stared at the fat man. "What else did you expect? This is a penal world not a nursery."

"But fifteen hundred left from over five thousand?" Laurance shook his head, his broad features reflecting his inner sickness. "One out of five! It's incredible!"

"Two out of seven," corrected Hogarth calmly.

"The percentage is increasing however and within a few months we hope to push it to fifty per cent. I doubt if it will be possible to salvage more than one man from every two."

"Why not? Is there disease here? If so, why didn't you inform the Federation? Is it the gravity? The environment? Suicide? What killed all those men?"

"Disease? No. Gravity? That has something to do with it and some men have committed suicide, but losses from that cause have been minor." Hogarth smiled. "I think you could say that it is due wholly to the environment."

"Then…" Laurance paused, his eyes thoughtful as he looked at the tall Admiral. He remembered half-forgotten tales of incidents during the war, of whispers ignored in the press of conflict, and he recalled a tall young man with a blue-scarred face whom he had watched beat a man to death. He nodded.

"Yes," he said quietly. "The environment. Of your making, of course?"

"Naturally."

"And you are proud of what you have done?"

"I am."

"Of course," Laurance said softly. "You would be. Almost four thousand men dead, and you are proud of what you have done. Incredible!"

"Why so?" Hogarth straightened in his chair and now he had lost his smile. "You sent me scum, the filth of the Federation, criminals and murderers to a man. Should I have nursed them? Babied them? Given them an opportunity to revolt and plan fresh horror? No, Laurance, I had a better plan. I took the wrecks you sent me and I moulded them with iron and fire. I weeded out the diseased, the drugged, the unsuitable. I filtered them and screened them and what is left represent the cream of them all."

"By murder?"

"No." Hogarth shrugged. "Some men have been shot, of course, discipline had to be enforced, but the majority died because they could not stand the pace. Out of the first four hundred prisoners only fifty survived, they are the sergeants, I believe that you saw one just before you came in."

"I did," said Laurance grimly. "A young man with a scarred face. He beat a man to death before my eyes."

"A scarred face?" Hogarth frowned. "I remember now. Wilson, a young man, the youngest we have, but full of promise and perfect officer material."

"Officer material?"

"Yes. Surely it is obvious to you that, in order to control the prisoners, I had to augment the guards? How else than by using selected prisoners themselves? The sergeants have been trained and tested in every way, and they are ready to take command of both weapons and men."

"Fifty sergeants?" Laurance shrugged. "That doesn't seem many to me."

"They are the sergeants," reminded Hogarth. "Then we have one hundred and fifty corporals and three hundred lance corporals. The other thousand are men who are in their last stages of training. They will be promoted when the new intake of prisoners has been weeded out and are ready for selected duties."

"Interesting," said the fat man drily. Hogarth didn't seem to notice his tone.

"We had to ease the training programme, of course, after the first batch had been processed, but the whole schedule is flexible and can be altered as the need arises. At the moment we are concentrating on toughening up the rankers, a new promotion schedule can be formulated as soon as the prisoner intake increases." He looked at the fat man. "When will that be?"

"Never."

"What! What do you mean?"

"Do you think that we are all as crazy as you are, Hogarth?" Laurance wiped sweat from his streaming features. "The Federation can't allow private armies, whether they are built by you or any other man. This insane programme has got to stop!"

"So?" Hogarth leaned back, his cold eyes watchful and bleak. "May I ask why? After all, what harm am I doing here? I am taking your unwanted scum and making men out of them. Admittedly

I am using a military regime to do it, but can you suggest a better alternative?"

"We can keep them apart, locked up in jails, isolated where they can do no harm."

"And keep them in comfort for the rest of their lives?" Hogarth sneered. "Is that the way to treat murderers?"

"Perhaps not," admitted Laurance. "But any alternative is better than your methods of rehabilitation." He leaned forward across the wide desk, his broad face earnest, his physical discomfort forgotten.

"Are you such a fool, Hogarth that you can't see what you are doing? These men are criminals, killers, convicted murderers. You have taken them, and, by sheer force and brutality, turned them into something resembling an army. But they are not an army, basically they are what they always have been. Scum! All you've done is to weed out the most savage of them, the most cold-blooded, the most dangerous. You're sitting on a volcano, Hogarth, the entire Federation is, and will be as long as these men have access to arms and freedom. What do they know of loyalty? Of patriotism? Of self-sacrifice? How can they even be expected to obey ethical laws and respect codes of conduct? No, Hogarth, this entire scheme must be brought to an end."

"No!"

"Yes!"

For a moment the two men glared at each other, and, on the tall Admiral's high forehead, little beads of sweat shone against the clear skin. He swallowed, seemed about to speak, then swallowed again.

"You are mistaken, Laurance," he said with forced calm. "You overlook one thing. You speak of loyalty and patriotism, but I have given them something just as good and far more effective than empty words and a vague dream. I have given them the Stellar Legion."

"So?"

"You are wrong in what you say. These men are loyal, not to Earth, not to the Federation or to an old-fashioned code of ethics, but to themselves. They have found the one thing that can unite them. The Legion!" He swallowed again, and dabbed irritably at the sweat trickling down his face.

"I have destroyed their basic contempt of authority. I have destroyed any possible hope of friendship between man and man. Each is a lone unit and each knows it. Instead of human friendship and personal loyalty they have the Legion. They are loyal to that because, in so doing, they are loyal to themselves. They are the Stellar Legion, and they know it, and nothing you can say or do will ever take that fact away from them."

"And what will they do when the Legion has been abolished?" Laurance shrugged. "Well, we can settle that problem when we come to it. In the meantime, this new batch of prisoners will be the last. The Federation cannot tolerate mass murder and potential enemies to the galactic peace."

"The Federation!" And this time Hogarth didn't trouble to hide his contempt. "A collection of starry-eyed innocents. They preach universal peace and think they can get it by the total abolition of arms. They are wrong, and, as an intelligent man, you should know it."

"Thank you," said the fat man quietly, "for admitting that I am an intelligent man I mean. But you are wrong, Hogarth. The Federation does not believe in a universal panacea for all ills. There are guns and there will always be guns, we know it, and we aren't worried. One man with a gun at his belt is relatively harmless, and we don't care how many quarrels there are, how many duels or riots. They are bad, but they can be tolerated. No. What we are against is the founding of any military force. One man is harmless, but a thousand men, led and guided by self-seekers and fools, can wreak irreparable harm. The Stellar Legion is such a force—and it must go!"

"Must it?" Hogarth shook his head. "No, Laurance. The Federation needs the Legion, despite what they say, they need it."

"No."

"Yes, Laurance, they do. What of raiders? You can't alter human nature and your petty police forces would be helpless to prevent a bold man gathering a crew and stealing a ship."

"Nonsense!"

"Is it, Laurance? Very well then. What of the Outside? What of the life forms that may lie out there—waiting?" Hogarth shrugged.

"I know that you don't believe in what I say, but I have better reason than all others for stating that the Legion cannot be abolished."

"And that is?"

"How are you going to do it?"

"Shut down the penal world. Cut off supplies. Stop..." The fat man paused, staring at the cold smile of the tall Admiral. "You wouldn't dare resist?"

"No?" Hogarth smiled, a thin smile, humourless and cold. "I am leader of the most highly trained and ruthless fighting force at present existing in the Federation of Man. You say it should be abolished. I differ." He leaned back in his chair. "Very well then, Laurance. Try and make me."

He chuckled at the expression on the fat man's sweating features.

CHAPTER 12

LAURANCE'S GAMBIT

Captain Rennie hitched at his heavy belt and glowered towards a line of sweating men. They stared back, their faces expressionless, and, as usual, the stocky captain felt his skin crawl to their radiated hate. Grimly he snapped terse commands.

"This is an elimination test. The winners will be in direct line for promotion. The losers..." He shrugged. "You've all had hypnotuition in armed and unarmed combat. Now. You're going to be divided in two parties and will face each other, man to man. One man will have a knife, the other be unarmed, and the trick is to win." He grinned. "I'm not too concerned how you win." His face hardened again. "One other thing. If any bright lad gets the idea of throwing a knife at one of the guards, he will be flayed, strung up by the heels, and left to die." He jerked his head towards Wilson. "Right. Issue the weapons."

Wilson nodded and picked up a basket full of glistening, ten-inch knives, each weapon razor sharp and needle pointed. He passed down the line, giving each second man a knife, and, at a snapped command, they fell apart and faced each other in pairs.

"Wait!" Rennie glanced at the young man. "Just to show you what I mean the sergeant will give a demonstration. Right, Wilson. Take your place."

For a split second Wilson hesitated, knowing that the stocky captain had no right to make him risk his neck in a routine elimination contest, and yet knowing at the same time that if he refused he would be shot down as an object lesson to the men. He shrugged, and gripping his club, stepped forward.

"Without the club, Wilson," snapped Rennie. "And unarmed."

Silently the young man threw his heavy club to the sand and took his place before a sweating, feral-eyed man. He remained outwardly calm, but deep within, he felt a rising hate towards the sadistic officer. He ignored it as he stared at his adversary.

The man was yellow-skinned, a native of the Sirian System, and for a moment Wilson was reminded of Conroy. He forced the memory into the background, and, muscles tensed waited for the word of command.

"Attack!"

The man weaved, sunlight splintering in bright shards from the long knife, and Wilson noted that he held it with a practised ease, thumb to the blade, the edge upwards, and the point raised. Such a hold prevented the simpler arm-locks, prevented also the sudden downward blow on the wrist, but equally so it meant that the man had no intention of throwing the blade.

Wilson waited, poised easily on the balls of his feet, watching for the first attack.

It came with a sudden rush and a warning flash of reflected sunlight. The man feinted, thrust, half-turned, and slashed in a sudden, vicious arc, the heavy air whining from the passage of the razor-edged steel.

Almost he got away with it. Almost the sudden, unexpected turn and slash, caught Wilson off guard, and pain burned a thin line just over his belt as he jerked away. Then they were facing each other again and blood oozed from a shallow gash across the young man's stomach.

Again the driving thrust, turning at the last moment into a withdrawing cut, aimed at severing clutching fingers or a reaching hand. Wilson avoided the trap, his left arm moving with deceptive speed as he dashed his wrist against the man's forearm. For a moment the threatening blade wavered, and, before the Sirian could recover his stance, Wilson stepped forward and jerked up his knee.

He missed!

Desperately he twisted as the steel lanced towards him, spinning on his heel, and throwing his weight to one side. He ducked, lunging forward and upwards beneath the flashing knife, and the back edge of the blade glanced harmlessly from his shoulder. Quickly he sprang forward, twisting to avoid an upthrust knee, jerking his head to one side as stiffened fingers stabbed at his eyes. He grunted, caught the knife arm in a reflex-dictated arm lock, and stooped forward, throwing the man over his hip. Bone snapped as the man hurtled through the heavy air, and he screamed once before he landed, head first, on the gritty sand. He landed, and lay still, his head at an odd angle to his body, his neck broken by the force of the impact beneath double gravity.

Wilson adjusted his cap and, picking up his club, looked at the stocky captain.

"Anything else, sir?"

"No. Get that wound dressed." Rennie turned to the watching men. "Right. Now let's see how you behave. Attack!"

Wilson strode away, his face expressionless, and behind him rose the animal-sounds of men engaged in desperate combat.

The doctor dressed his wound, spraying a clear, hormone-rich plastic over the shallow cut, the transparent, antiseptic plastic hardening into a flexible film, numbing with its anaesthetic properties.

A fat man called to him as he left the medical quarters, and Wilson halted, staring at the civilian with bleak eyes.

"You're Wilson aren't you?"

"Yes."

"My name is Laurance, I'm a Director of the Federation of Man."

"I know. We've met before."

"So we have." Laurance grinned. "I thought that perhaps you'd forgotten." He glanced around, staring distastefully at the struggling men on the training grounds and the watchful guards. "I want to talk to you. Is there anywhere we can go?"

"What's wrong with where we are?"

"Nothing, but this is a private matter. Can we go somewhere secluded?"

Wilson hesitated, frowning at the fat man, and half undecided whether or not this was some new test, a subtle trap to get him alone and at a disadvantage. Laurance seemed able to read his thoughts.

"I mean you no harm," he said quietly. "I'm not interested in promotion and you have nothing to fear from me. Well?"

"We can talk as we walk," snapped the young man. He led the way on a wide circle around the settlement, oblivious to the discomfort of the man at his side. Laurance gasped, struggling to move his increased weight, and caught the young man by the arm.

"Not so fast, Wilson. I'm not as young as you are." He stared curiously at the tall figure. "Just how old are you, anyway?"

"Nineteen, almost. Why?"

"So young?" Laurance sucked in his breath. "Been here long?"

"A year."

"One of the first, eh?"

"Yes."

"Like it?"

Wilson didn't answer, but stared hard at the fat man at his side. Laurance smiled.

"No, I'm not trying to trap you or anything like that." His voice grew hard. "I asked you a question. Answer it!"

"Go to hell!"

"So?" Laurance nodded as if proving some particular point, and, when he spoke, his voice had the harsh tones of one used to command. "Listen. I want you to realise who I am. I am a Director of the Federation. Do you know what that is?"

"Yes."

"Good. Then you know that I am more powerful than any other man on this planet. More powerful than you, or your officers, or Hogarth himself. I want you to believe that. Do you?"

"No." Wilson stared at the round face of the fat man. "I could kill you," he said coldly. "Could you kill me?"

"I could order your death."

"Could you?" Wilson drew back his lips in a tight line and his hand shifted on the club swinging at his wrist. Laurance shrugged.

"Oh, you could kill me, I don't doubt it, but what would it get you?" He smiled up at the tall young man. "Killing doesn't get you anywhere, son. Haven't you learned that yet?"

"It got me promotion."

"So? And what else?"

"It got me sent here," said Wilson tightly. He stared over the sun-baked desert. "Is that all you've got to say to me?"

"No." Laurance halted and stared seriously at the young man. "I want to offer you something better than anything you've ever had in your life before. I want to see whether you're intelligent enough to realise what you're up against and what must happen to you if you don't obey me."

"Obey you?"

"Yes. I am your superior. I am Hogarth's superior and that means he must do as I say."

"Then why talk to me?"

Laurance didn't answer, but slowly began to walk towards the swollen ball of the giant sun. Wilson hesitated for a moment, then, his curiosity aroused, strode after him. For a while they walked in silence, the sounds from the settlement growing fainter as they left it far behind, then the fat man plumped down on a heat-blistered rock and mopped his streaming face.

"Tell me, Wilson," he said quietly. "What happens if you refuse to obey an order?"

"Death."

"I see. And if you should kill a guard?"

"The same." Wilson swallowed and sat down beside the fat man. "It happened once. A column of men, fifty or so, were out on a march and one of them killed a guard."

"What happened? Did they kill the man responsible?"

"No. They killed him right enough, but not at once. They flayed him and rubbed him with sand then they strung him up by the heels to die. He was a long time dying. Then they took the rest of the column and shot them down. They did it before all the men, and afterwards, when it was all over, they made us clean up the mess." Wilson paused. "That was the only guard to die," he said slowly.

"I see." Laurance thinned his lips. "So, if Hogarth should disobey his superiors, it is logical to you that he should be made to suffer, and, not only him, but all those in his command." He stared at the young man. "All of you," he said deliberately. "Can you see what I mean?"

"I'm not sure," said Wilson slowly. He stared down at the sand between his feet. "Who would do the punishing?"

"The Federation of Man."

"With what?"

"Atomic bombs!"

Laurance smiled with quiet satisfaction at the young man's involuntary reaction at the sound of that which had caused him so much pain and misery. He had counted on it, the blue scar was obvious proof that at one time Wilson had been caught in a radiant area, and to such men the very thought of atomics was repellant. Grimly he pressed his advantage.

"One bomb," he said softly. "Blasting and searing the entire settlement with radioactive destruction. Have you even seen the effects of such a bomb? Can you imagine it? The heat and pain, the burned stench of seared flesh, the agony and the shamble of men blinded and crippled, scarred and twisted, crawling on stumps of limbs, crying for help, crying..."

"Stop it!" Wilson shuddered, great beads of sweat glistening on his hard features. "Stop it I tell you!"

"Nasty, isn't it," whispered Laurance. "But it can happen, Wilson. It will happen unless Hogarth comes to his senses and obeys his superiors. Just as you would be shot down for refusing to obey an order, just as that man was tortured and his fellows murdered, so Hogarth and every man on this planet will be wiped out unless you do as I say." He paused, staring at the young man, afraid to say too much and so defeat his own object, and yet fighting the temptation to keep talking and to pile fuel on Wilson's inner torment. He bit his lips, forcing himself to look away, towards the ochre desert and the flaring ball of Capella blazing in awful splendour low on the horizon.

Next to him Wilson sat, frowning in thought, fighting an inner battle with the twin conditioning imposed by his rigorous training. To obey and survive. Obey and survive! To refuse to obey meant death, for, in a thousand ways and with many examples, the lesson had been driven home. But if to obey meant death also? He shuddered and, moving as if by its own volition, his hand touched the ugly scar mottling his cheek,

"How can I believe you?" he whispered. "How can I be sure?"

Laurance sighed, schooling his features and hiding his relief, and when he stared at the young man his broad features were devoid of emotion.

"I am a Director of the Federation," he said quietly. "Why should I lie?"

"But Hogarth?"

"He is a madman. He will lead you only to death, is leading you to death, for, unless he obeys me, Stellar will be destroyed."

"I don't believe you."

"Suit yourself." Laurance shrugged and rose from his seat. "Shall we go back now?"

"Yes." Wilson joined him and together they began the long walk back to the settlement.

Laurance didn't look at the young man as they walked but kept his eyes steadily before him He wasn't worried. The thought had been planted, the seed sown, and time and ingrained conditioning would do the rest. He wasn't surprised when Wilson spoke.

"If I do obey you, what would happen to me?"

"Nothing."

"Nothing?"

Laurance caught the note of surprise and cursed himself for a fool. He should have known by what he had seen and learned that the settlement was run on a system of reward and punishment. To swing the young man fully to his purpose he would have to increase the incentive to survive. But he had been thrown off by the phrasing of the question.

"If you help me," he said deliberately, "I will see to it that you receive a full pardon, a cash grant, and transportation to any planet you may care to name." He looked at the young man. "You know the alternative."

"Yes," said Wilson, and bit his lip, his grey eyes thoughtful.

The fat man could be telling the truth in which case his course of action was obvious. Aside from any monetary reward his first duty was to survive, and, if betraying Hogarth meant survival, then the tall Admiral would have to go. But if the fat man were lying? Wilson frowned as he puzzled it out. The penalty of disobedience was death, swift, sudden, irrevocable, and Wilson had no intention of dying. As yet he had obeyed every order and he was safe, but the threat of atomic weapons on Stellar was a grim one, and if Laurance was a Director of the Federation, and he seemed to have authority, then what?

It was a problem, a bad one, one that couldn't be solved by ruthless action and savage violence, and Wilson felt at a loss. He needed more data.

"Why did you pick on me?" he asked. "Why tell me all this?"

"Does that matter?" Laurance stumbled over a stone and almost fell, grunting as he cautiously tested his ankle for strain. "Do you want to die?"

"No."

"Then you will take what I offer? The money, the pardon and the rest?"

"Perhaps."

"You surprise me," said Laurance slowly. "Don't you want to get back home? Rejoin your parents and friends, make a decent life for yourself and forget all this man-made hell?"

"Home means nothing to me and I have no parents or friends." Wilson kicked at a piece of crumbling rock. "What good would money be to me and where would I go? Here I feel at home." He stared at the fat man. "Does the Federation have an army? Could I join it?"

"No," said Laurance, and immediately cursed himself for a fool. Desperately he tried to cover the mistake. "I mean that we don't have an army, not that you couldn't join it, but there is the police force and plenty of frontier planets where you could settle."

"You don't have an army?" Wilson ignored the rest of the fat man's words, concentrating on the one important factor. "Then you lied! Without an army how could you bomb Stellar?"

"I said we had no army," Laurance tried to force conviction into his voice. "But we have plenty of ships and there are still bombs in storage. It would only take one, remember, just one medium-sized atomic bomb and Stellar would be a thing of the past."

He halted on the edge of the settlement and Wilson became conscious of curious eyes staring at him from the shadow of visored caps.

"In any case," said Laurance easily. "You don't have much choice now, do you?"

"What do you mean?"

"The guards have seen you talking to me. They know that we were alone together for a long time out of observation. They will suspect you, Wilson, and you know what happens to men they suspect." He smiled. "Better stand by me when the time comes, if you don't, I don't think that you're going to live very long."

He turned, a fat, somehow ludicrous man, and watching him go, Wilson felt a surge of frustrated anger.

He should have killed the man when he'd had the chance.

CHAPTER 13

ULTIMATUM

Admiral Hogarth sat in his office and listened to the muted words whispering from the ultra beam receiver snug against the bone behind his ear. He smiled, and, pressing a button in his pocket, broke the connection.

He glanced up as Rennie entered the room.

The stocky captain looked worried, his heavy brows creased in an unusual frown, and his grey uniform was more rumpled and dusty than normal. He slumped, uninvited, into a chair.

"How long's this Laurance going to hang around?"

Hogarth shrugged, a peculiar expression in his pale, washed-out blue eyes. "Until he finally decides to go back home I suppose. Why do you ask?"

"I don't like him here, that's why. I've a feeling he's trying to cause trouble."

"Indeed?" Hogarth relaxed, his slender fingers resting on the edge of an open drawer. "Has he been talking to you?"

"Yes." Rennie glared defiantly at the tall Admiral. "And I'm not the only one. He's been talking to some of the prisoners, the doctor, Dewer as well, and what he says doesn't make good hearing."

"No?"

"No. He talks sense and I'm worried."

"You're a fool," said Hogarth emotionlessly. "A timid fool frightened of shadows. You should know better."

"Should I?" Rennie wiped sweat from his swarthy features. "Like it or not, Laurance is from the Federation, and the man has power. If he wished he could cut off all our supplies, blockade the planet, and that isn't all. He's threatened..."

"I know what he's threatened," snapped Hogarth sharply. "But that is all he has done, threaten." He glanced irritably towards the opening door. "What is it?"

"Please, sir," stammered a grey-uniformed guard with the double stripe of a corporal. "Director Laurance insists on seeing you."

"Does he?" Hogarth frowned then wiped his face clean of emotion as the fat man thrust his way past the guard. "Really, Laurance, I happen to be very busy."

"You'll see me," said the fat man coldly. He glanced at Rennie. "You may as well stay and hear what has to be said."

"Is this an ultimatum, Laurance?"

"Did I say that, Hogarth?" The fat man slumped into a chair. "But I intend leaving soon, in a matter of hours, and I should like to clear up a few things before I go."

"Leaving?"

"That's what I said." Laurance dabbed at his streaming face. "And don't get any wrong ideas, Hogarth. I am in constant ultra beam communication with my ship. It would be most unwise to hold me against my will."

"Hold you?" Hogarth smiled. "What a fantastic idea! Surely, Laurance, you don't think that I would be as foolish as that?"

"I think that you're fool enough for almost anything," said the fat man with quiet deliberation. "Even now I can't believe that you aren't aware of what you've done." He glanced around the cool room. "I think it would be wise to ask the other of your officers here. You have a doctor, I know, and a psychologist, too, I believe. Are there any others?"

"No," said Hogarth hastily, and glanced at Rennie. "Would you get them for me please, Captain. I assume that the matter is urgent?"

"It is," said Laurance grimly. "And while you're at it, fetch Wilson here, too."

"Sergeant Wilson?"

"Yes." The fat man stared curiously at the tall Admiral. "I want to prove something to you, something you seem to have deliberately overlooked, and that young man will serve as well as any other for an object lesson." He narrowed his eyes at the Admiral's hesitation. "I insist, Hogarth!"

Hogarth shrugged, as a man might shrug who humours a troublesome child, giving way secure in the knowledge that he can end the farce whenever he so wishes. He nodded to the waiting captain, and, after the man had gone, relaxed in his chair, his hand thrust deep in his pocket, a thin, half-smile on his cruel mouth.

Rennie didn't take long.

He ushered in the bleak-faced doctor and the little psychologist, and rapped sharp orders to the tall young man at his side.

"Stand over by the wall, Wilson."

"Yes, sir." The young man crossed the room and stood, watching, the blue scar on his cheek an ugly blotch against his tan. Laurance sighed.

"First," he said quietly. "You all know why I'm here. The Federation cannot tolerate the existence of such a force as this, and so, it must be abolished. So far, so good, but Admiral Hogarth does not agree with either me or the Federation. I am curious to find out why."

"You know why," snapped Hogarth. "Need we go into all that again?"

"No, it is hardly necessary, but I refuse to credit that you are so blind as not to know what you have done." The fat man leaned forward in his chair. "I can understand why you did it, of course, the military mind is a surprisingly uncomplicated mechanism, but did you have to be so blind?"

"What do you mean?" Hogarth let his pale eyes flicker over the silent men. "What am I supposed to have done?"

Laurance hid his smile and waited, letting the silence deepen and the tension mount as the listeners strained for his answer. Then, at just the right moment, he spoke.

"You have sown the seeds of your own destruction," he said quietly, and leaned back, waiting for the explosion.

Hogarth laughed.

It was a dry sound, like the rustle of dry leaves as they whispered in the evening of the dying year, and it echoed through the silent room as the rattle of bleached bones might sound in a deserted graveyard. It was an old man's laugh, the vocal humour of one who had almost forgotten what humour was, and the watching men felt their skin crawl at the alien sound.

"You fool!" he said, and wiped at his pale eyes. "You poor, blind, helpless fool." He laughed again, and Rennie, whether from nervousness of trained reflex action laughed with him, his deep guffaw drowning the thin cackle. Laurance did not laugh, nor the doctor, nor Wilson, and the little psychologist bit his thin lips as he stared first at the fat man, then at the tall Admiral.

He seemed worried.

"So you think that do you?" Hogarth recovered his icy calm and glanced at the still sniggering captain. Rennie gulped and became suddenly grave. "So you think that I've sown the seeds of my own destruction." He paused. "A nice phrase that, but, like most nice phrases, hopelessly untrue."

"You think so?" Laurance shrugged. "Well, there are none so blind as those who will not see." He let his eyes drift to the doctor, the silent figure against the wall, the little psychologist, then back to Wilson again. He ignored Rennie.

"I have been interested in your system of training," he said evenly, almost as though he discussed the weather. "You seem to have operated on two motivations, obedience and survival." He stared at the tall Admiral. "The first I can understand, but why the second?"

"A good soldier is one who can save his own life and live to fight again."

"Do you really believe that?" Laurance shrugged. "How then do you reconcile it with the first?"

"Obedience?" Hogarth snorted with sudden impatience. "Of what use is a soldier who cannot obey?"

"None, but then, the average soldier is one who obeys and nothing else."

"Not the men of the Stellar Legion. They are far from average."

"Yes," said Laurance, and his eyes flickered to the tall figure standing against the wall. "You speak greater truth than you know." He stared at Hogarth.

"Your dream of a select group of perfect soldiers isn't a new one. Probably the first we know of were the Spartans, and, in later times, there were the commandoes, the rangers, the paratroops and suicide squadrons. All consisted of relatively small, highly trained groups of men, but, with the possible exception of the Spartans, they all had one thing in common, one thing which you do not have."

"And that is?"

"They were all volunteers."

"So?"

"So they wanted to do what they did. They were fired by patriotism and loyalty and they suffered hardship gladly because of that fact. Even in the total wars of history, at a time when almost every man and woman had been conscripted to the military machine, those groups always consisted of those who wanted to join them. Is the Stellar Legion like that?"

"The Legion is what I've made it," snapped Hogarth. "I did what I could with the material I had."

"And what material!" The fat man shrugged. "Criminals the lot of them, killers, murderers, convicted and sent here for rehabilitation. Each one of them hated being sent here, hated what they had to do and more than hated those who made them do it. Loyalty? Patriotism? Self-sacrifice? They have none of it, and why should they?"

"They are loyal to the Legion."

"Yes, you said that before, but are they? How do you know?"

"They must be. Dewer..." Hogarth swallowed and forced himself to be calm. "They are loyal to the Legion because they have nothing else to be loyal to."

"I see, a perfect example of illogical reasoning, but why should you think that such a loyalty is a good thing? It isn't you know. There is only one good loyalty, and that isn't to the patch of ground on which you happened to be born, the culture of which you happen to be a part, or to those whose company you keep. There is only one loyalty, and that is to Mankind. All of Mankind, not just a part of it, loyalty to the human race!"

"Idealist!" sneered Hogarth.

"Yes," admitted Laurance. "I'm an idealist. I happen to believe in peace for all, not just for those with the same coloured skin as myself, or for those who think as I do. That belief founded the Federation of Man, and no power-mad fool of a broken-down Admiral is going to threaten it!"

He paused, half amazed at himself for displaying so much emotion and surprised that he could feel so deeply over, what was after all, almost an abstract idea. He shook his head and changed the subject, recognising the danger of straying from his chosen path.

"You have tried to do the impossible, Hogarth, and you have failed as you were doomed to fail."

"Have I?" The tall Admiral tilted his head a little and his hand moved in his pocket as he closed the connection on the portable ultra beam equipment. "In just which way?"

"You have taken men and tried to instil them with dual, conflicting motivations. Survive and obey. A soldier shouldn't even think of survival, Hogarth. His duty is to obey, purely and simply, without thought or question. How else can you expect him to attack overwhelming odds? How else can a thinking creature rush into the face of terrible death? Soldiers shouldn't even be able to think for themselves, and, in the old days, they knew that. Discipline was founded on the simple necessity that to be of use a soldier had to have his spirit broken on the wheel of dull, stupid, monotonous routine. His officers knew that they had to crush his initiative, his survival instinct, and his belligerence, for, unless they did so, he would rebel at thrusting himself into certain death."

Laurance stared at the tall Admiral and frowned. He had the impression that something was going on of which he had no knowledge, and the impression worried him. Grimly he continued.

"And so I say that you have sown the seeds of your own destruction. These men you have trained are here because they had no choice. They have been weeded out on a survival basis, and they are strict individuals." He leaned over the wide desk. "What is going to happen when you give a contra-survival order?"

"They will obey!"

"Will they?" Laurance shook his head. "I doubt it, why should they?"

"They have always obeyed," said Hogarth grimly. "And they always will."

"No. They have obeyed up to now because to obey meant to survive, but this time it is different, to obey you now means to die." He stared grimly at the Admiral. "You don't believe me? Then I shall prove it."

"How?" snapped Hogarth, and in his chair the little psychologist gnawed at his knuckles with a sudden, uncontrollable nervousness. The doctor said nothing but his eyes were very bright and watchful. Rennie shifted a little, his hands automatically adjusting the belt around his waist, his lips pursed in indecision.

Laurance pointed at Wilson.

"Come over here."

The tall young man hesitated, glancing at the captain, then, at Rennie's curt nod, crossed the room with long, easy strides.

"Yes, sir?"

"At ease," snapped Rennie.

"I have chosen Wilson for this experiment," said Laurance easily, "because he is the youngest man on the planet, he has been here since the penal colony was established, and because he is a sergeant. Three reasons which make him ideal for this test. He is young enough so that he must have been relatively free of any prior conditioning, and, the fact that he is a sergeant, must signify that he is a successful result of your training methods. Do you agree?"

"Yes," said Hogarth, and despite himself he felt interested. "What are you trying to prove?"

"You admit then that Wilson must be representative of your methods? In other words, the characteristics he displays must be true of the rest of the group in general. Do you admit that?"

"Yes." Hogarth glanced at the tense features of the little psychologist. "Wilson is a good man."

"Exactly. The type of man you have tried so hard to produce. Tough and hard, ruthless and in perfect physical form. A cold-blooded fighting machine—and utterly selfish in having a strong survival instinct. The type of man of which you have produced fifteen hundred so far. The men of the Stellar Legion."

He glanced at the tall young man.

"I've said all this before him so that there can be no possibility of conditioned reflex. I don't want that type of reaction at all. I want to see whether a logical, reasoning being, with a high survival factor, is or can be, your ideal of the perfect soldier."

"I follow your argument," snapped Hogarth impatiently. "Get on with it."

"Right." Laurance stared at the stocky captain. "Give him your gun."

"What?"

"Do as I say. Give him your gun." The fat man smiled at the captain's hesitation. "So. Could it be that you daren't trust your soldiers with weapons?"

"Give him the gun, Rennie," Hogarth snapped irritably. The captain shrugged and unsheathed the gleaming pistol. Wilson didn't move.

"Take it!"

"Yes sir." The tall young man took the weapon and stood, poising it expertly in his hand.

"I see that you've had weapon training," mused Laurance. "Very well then. Kill yourself!"

Wilson didn't alter his position, but now the gun had levelled in his hand, the slender barrel menacing the fat man.

"You refuse?" Laurance shrugged and stared at the tall Admiral. "You see?"

"What of it? What thinking man would kill himself because of an order?"

"It has been known," said Laurance quietly. "It is recorded history that several old-time commanders had troops who would leap over the edge of a cliff at a word of command. But never mind that. You noted that I ordered him to kill, not shoot himself. It is barely possible that he would wound himself if his survival depended on it, but tell me this Hogarth, what is the difference between ordering a man to kill himself and ordering him on a suicidal mission?" .

"No mission is so suicidal that there isn't the possibility of escape."

"And yet the Kami-Kazt pilots of the second world war had no possible hope of escape and they obeyed the order to launch themselves and their piloted bombs against the enemy." Laurance smiled at the expression on the Admiral's thin features, then, with shocking abruptness, his voice altered.

It became hard and cold, bleak and chilled with grim finality and inborn authority. It rang against the walls and echoed flatly around the room, and, hearing it, Rennie recognised Laurance for what he was. Not a fat and stupid-looking man, but a thing of iron and ice, grim and relentless, a man who had watched entire planets smoulder in atomic destruction so that an ancient dream of a united mankind could arise from the ashes of bitter hate.

"Let us finish this play," he snapped. "You all know who I am, a Director of the Federation of Man, and, as that, I am as far above Hogarth as he is above the meanest prisoner. He must obey me as you must obey him. If he does not, then he will be punished, and you will be punished with him." He paused and, in the silence, the sounds of men breathing sounded strangely loud.

"I order you to relinquish your command, Hogarth. I order it in the name of the Federation!"

For a moment he hoped that the tall Admiral would give way, that he would see reason and logic, acceptingly and gracefully what must be, then, as he saw the thin features harden, he knew that he had to depend-on others.

"Do you refuse?"

"Yes," said Hogarth stubbornly. "I refuse."

Laurance sighed, his head slumping forward on his chest, and his lips moved as if in silent prayer. He straightened, his eyes cold, and stared at the young man with the blue scar.

"Unless you relinquish your command, Hogarth, the Federation will take it as an act of rebellion against the galactic peace. The penalty is death. Death for you and all on this planet."

"Including yourself!" Hogarth didn't trouble to hide his sneer. "You're bluffing!"

"No, Hogarth, I'm mot bluffing. I mean exactly what I say. Unless you surrender your command I shall order atomic missiles to be fired at Stellar from my ship orbiting the planet."

"You wouldn't dare!"

"I refuse to argue with you, Hogarth. You know that I can do what I say, and you know that you are beaten. To destroy all life on this world would be a terrible thing, but better that than permit a madman with a mad ideal to range the Federation. We cannot permit that, Hogarth, and you know it."

"I know that you wouldn't dare to bomb Stellar. What of the prisoners?"

"They will die." Laurance stared at the tall Admiral. "Do you doubt my ability to fulfil my threat?"

"You could bomb us right enough," snapped Hogarth. "But..." He gulped, his words fading into silence, his thin features the colour of putty, his eyes wide and startled with something more than mere fear. He recoiled, his hand clawing at the half-open drawer of his desk, then snatched it away in frantic terror.

Wilson stared at him, Rennie's forgotten weapon levelled at the shrinking body of the tall Admiral.

CHAPTER 14

TRAITOR'S END

For a long moment no one moved or spoke, and, the pistol in Wilson's hand never wavered as he levelled it at the tall Admiral's stomach. Hogarth gulped, his pale eyes flickering from face to face.

"Put down that gun!" he snapped desperately "Rennie!"

"Don't move," said Wilson coldly. He stepped back to a point where he could cover the entire group. He glanced at Laurance. "Call off your ship. Hogarth has surrendered his command."

"No!" Hogarth half-swayed towards the open drawer then recoiled as light gleamed from the barrel of the pistol. "You don't know what you're doing, Wilson. Laurance is bluffing."

"You admitted that he could bomb us all."

"I know, but..."

"I don't want to die," said Wilson grimly. If he has the power to bomb us then we wouldn't stand a chance against him." He stared at the fat man. "Call your ship and order them to withdraw."

"You fool!" Anger made the tall Admiral quiver with frustrated rage. "He hasn't got a ship. He was bluffing all the time."

"Call your ship," repeated the young man and Laurance obediently lowered his head, his lips moving silently as he spoke into the concealed throat microphone of an ultra beam transmitter. He smiled at the baffled face of the Admiral.

"Well, Hogarth. Have I proved my point?"

"You've proved nothing except that I'm surrounded by traitors and fools. Damn you. Laurance. What do you hope to gain by all this?"

"Isn't it obvious?" The fat man smiled as he leaned back in his chair. "Where is this loyalty you keep talking about? This adherence to the Stellar Legion? You admitted that Wilson was a representative of what you have bred here, and yet, at the first threat to his personal safety, he turned on you. He turned as any of the others would turn. He turned because he couldn't help it, because you have bred in him a high regard for his own skin. Why should he die to save your neck?"

"I am his commander," said Hogarth sickly. "He should have stood be me."

"But he didn't." Laurance stared at the stocky captain. "Well, Rennie? Are you satisfied?"

"I've always known it," grunted the short man. "I've felt it every time I've moved among them. Hate. Hate and fear. I tried to tell Hogarth what was happening but he wouldn't listen. He knew best, him and his damn psychologist. I tell you that I wouldn't go into battle with a bunch of prisoners if the fate of Earth depended on it. They'd kill me and desert at the first opportunity." He spat. "Hogarth is a fool."

"Rennie!" Ice crackled in the tall Admiral's voice. "How dare you! You, a captain of the Legion to address me so." He glared at Wilson. "Kill him! Kill him and his rank is yours!"

Wilson hesitated, the gun shifting in his hand, his grey eyes cold as he stared at the stocky captain. Rennie gulped, his hand dropping to his empty holster, and looked appealingly at the fat man. Laurance shook his head.

"He won't kill you, Rennie. His survival doesn't depend on it and so there is no reason why he should." He looked, almost pityingly, at the tall Admiral. "Can't you recognise when you're beaten, Hogarth? None of these men will obey you once they know that obedience means their own death."

"They will obey," said Hogarth grimly. He stared at the weapon in the young man's hand. "Put that thing away!"

"Relax, Wilson," ordered the fat man calmly. "Just stand and watch." He sighed. "A perfect example of conditioned reflex," he mused. "Press the right buttons and he will react in a predictable way. Your psychologist, Hogarth, must be a very clever man."

"Yes," said the Admiral, and a muscle jerked high on one cheek. "A very clever man." He picked up a small ornamental knife lying on his desk and looked at Dewer. "You did this," he said thickly. "You told me..."

"What if I did?" A change had come over the little man. He sat, glaring defiantly at the tall figure, and little trickles of saliva ran from the corners of his twitching mouth.

"You thought that you were clever, Hogarth. You thought that you could treat me like a dog, like some strange cur, and at the same time you expected me to be loyal to you. Well, now you see the result." He sniggered, a high-pitched, unhealthy tittering. "I've beaten you, Hogarth. I've shown you just what brains can do. Try using your guns now. Try calling your guards, those you have left here, and make me undo what I've done." He gulped and the trickle of saliva increased to a copious flow.

"I've surrounded you with enemies, with men who hate and fear you, who will kill you at the first opportunity. How do you like that, Hogarth? What does it feel like to be the most hated man on an entire world?" He spat with sudden, vicious anger. "You damn martinet! Strutting and acting the God. Who the hell are you anyway? A trained murderer, a destroyer, worse than the scum you asked me to train into men. Well, I trained them for you. I made them obey but I did more than that. I made them survive." He tittered again and the expression on Hogarth's face was that of a man who stared directly into hell.

"You swine!" he said, and the little knife jerked in his hand. "You dirty little swine!"

"So I'm a swine am I?" Dewer snarled, baring his uneven teeth, looking like a cornered rat as he crouched in the chair. "Swine or not I've beaten ,you, Hogarth. See what your shouting and strutting will do for you now."

"So you planned all this?" Laurance stared at the distorted face of the little man. Dewer grinned.

"I did," he giggled. "But you spoiled it all. I wanted to see his face when he ordered the men to attack against hopeless odds. They would have refused, you know, turned on him and left him a broken old man. Then, when that happened, he would have thought of me, of Dewer the man he treated worse than a dog."

He tittered again, the unhealthy sound rising into a shrieking outburst of hysterical, insane amusement, and pointed a thin finger at the rigid figure of the grim-faced Admiral.

"Look at him! Look at the potential Emperor of Earth! Playing with his poor fools of soldiers like some demented child playing with its toys. Look…"

He choked, his eyes starting from his head, and his thin hands clawed at his throat, at the gushing blood and the ornamental hilt of the small knife protruding like a strange growth from the side of his neck.

Quickly the doctor stepped to his side, his chair crashing over as he rose, and shook his head as he examined the wound.

"Not a chance. It's slashed the jugular."

Dewer gurgled, his thin legs thrashing as he fought against the rising tides of blackness obliterating his universe. He twitched, tried to speak, then sank back, his starting eyes glazed and his limp, blood-stained hands falling from his ruined throat.

Silently the doctor closed the horrible eyes and folded the lifeless hands.

"He's dead." He stared at Hogarth as if seeing him for the first time. "You killed him!"

"It was an accident," stammered the tall Admiral. "He goaded me too far. I had the knife in my hand, and…" He shook his head and regained something of his usual calm. "He tricked me," he muttered. "He deserved to die."

"But not like that." The doctor shook his head. "You had no right to kill him, Hogarth. It was murder!"

"It was justice!" Hogarth drew a deep breath and shrugged. "What is one death more or less? Dewer was a traitor, you all heard what he said, and he died a traitor's death. Forget it."

"No," said Laurance quietly. "We can't forget it." He rose to his feet. "Hogarth, you have just murdered a man, and murdered him before witnesses. Do I have to tell you the penalty of murder?"

"It was no murder," snapped the tall Admiral. "Dewer was insane."

"Even an insane man has some right."

"This is ludicrous," Hogarth snapped. "Many men have died on Stellar. Thousands of men. What does one more matter?"

"How many men have you killed, Hogarth?" Laurance ignored the sweat trickling over his broad features. "You have ordered the deaths of many, but how many have you personally killed?"

"None," snapped Rennie. "He only gave the orders."

"Some of the prisoners were shot," admitted Hogarth. "And I gave the orders, but what of it? I was given a free hand and it was essential to maintain discipline."

"Perhaps, and I'm not arguing about the past, but this time it's different. This time it wasn't some poor devil of a prisoner who was shot down at your orders, but one of your own men. A man with rights and beneath the full protection of the law!"

"He was a soldier and I his commanding officer. I have a right to punish my own men."

"There is no army here," reminded Laurance grimly. "This is a penal world and all on it are civilians, free men with the exception of the prisoners. Even if they were soldiers, still you couldn't murder them with impunity." He paused, and when he spoke his voice was an accusation.

"You murdered Dewer!"

"I punished him."

"You killed him, murdered him before witnesses, and there was no possible justification for the crime." The fat man sucked in a deep breath. "Hogarth. In the name of the Federation of Man I arrest you for the murder of Dewer. You will be taken from this place and taken to a recognised place of trial." He looked steadily at the tall Admiral. "I need hardly tell you what happens to convicted murderers."

It was only then that the full irony of the situation struck the watching men. Laurance had been clever, diabolically clever, using the duel training of the trained men to reveal the subtle treachery of the little psychologist. Then Hogarth had let his emotions betray him in vengeful action, an action which would strip him of rank and send him straight back to Stellar.

To the bottom of his own, man-made hell!

Hogarth stood, his pale, washed-out blue eyes flickering over the watching men, then incredibly, he smiled.

"Very clever," he said calmly, and sat down behind the wide desk. "It is a pity that, as a law-abiding man, you are at such a disadvantage."

Laurance frowned, again conscious of the feeling that there was something hidden, something he didn't know. Things had been too easy, had gone too closely to plan, and, with instinctive caution, he began to search for the flaw in his own logic.

"The trouble with all law-abiding people," said Hogarth easily, "is that they are so helpless when dealing with those who don't give that for law and order." He snapped his fingers. "Your directives and regulations can only work while everyone agrees to abide by them. If I were such a man I would surrender to your powers of arrest, stand my trial with its inevitable result, and come back here to commence my training." His voice hardened. "But I'm not such a man, Laurance, and you are a fool to imagine that I am."

"I can enforce my arrest," said the fat man quietly. Hogarth shrugged.

"So this is to be a trial of strength then? Good." He smiled. "Rather here, on my own planet, than somewhere in space or on a Federation world." He leaned back in his chair, surprisingly at his ease. "Well, Laurance? What now?"

"I shall call my ship and have you taken to a Federation world. You know what to expect then, Hogarth, and you know that we have the power to enforce our decrees."

"No." Hogarth straightened in his chair. "You only imagine that you have the power, but never mind that now," He smiled. "And what do you intend doing with the men I have trained? Turn them loose on an unsuspecting galaxy? Hold them here until they die? Tell me, Laurance, what do you intend doing with them?"

"We shall find a way," snapped the fat man, and his eyes drifted towards the tall, silent figure against the wall. "They will be found suitable employment."

"Yes," mused Hogarth. "You probably could at that. There is always a use for such men, perhaps opening new worlds and extending the known frontiers, perhaps even, you could assimilate them into the police." He chuckled. "You know the old adage."

"I know it," said Lauranee. He glanced at Wilson. "This has gone on long enough. I must ask you to submit, Hogarth, I do not wish to use force."

"Submit?" Hogarth shrugged. "You are an optimist, Laurance. You think, that because you have persuaded one of my men to turn against me, I am helpless. You are wrong. Wilson reported your conversation to me immediately you left him, and, as soon as he knows that you are helpless, he will be back at my side."

"But Dewer..."

"Dewer was a traitorous dog, but I have handled mutinous troops before. Let them see the glint of gold and handle loot, the sack of planets and the thrill of combat, and they will unite and be loyal. There is nothing like an action or two to solidify raw men. I know men, Laurance, and I know what they want. These men will stop at nothing, for, only too well, they know that only in the Legion could they be safe from paying the penalties of their crimes." Hogarth chuckled. "Beginning to feel worried, Laurance?"

"Should I?"

"Why not?" The tall Admiral relaxed in his chair. "Hasn't it occurred to you that all this has been just a little too easy? Why do you think I allowed you to land here, to question my guards and prisoners, rove over the settlement and try to turn my men against me?" He shrugged. "I will admit that you have pointed out a weakness and I thank you for it. I must thank you too for exposing Dewer's betrayal of his trust, but I am a military man, Laurance, and men of my calibre are used to taking a few elementary precautions." Contempt chilled his voice.

"Were you such a fool as to think you could walk in here, say a few words, and walk out again with me as your prisoner? Believe me, Laurance, if that had been the case you would never have lived for an hour on Stellar."

Laurance felt a swift return of his former fears. He stared at Wilson and jerked his head.

"Take the Admiral to his quarters and lock him up."

Wilson didn't move and Hogarth shrugged.

"The farce is almost over, Laurance. I must remind you that an astute commander must know his own strength." He chuckled again and the fat man felt perspiration start from his broad features. This was it! This was the thing he had been waiting for, the thing he had been afraid of, the unknown factor in this game of human chess.

"You have an ultra beam transmitter, Laurance, and so have I. The portable kind, of course, I can see the receiver just behind your ear, but then such a man as you would know just how far to bluff." Hogarth smiled, he seemed to be enjoying himself and the fat man glanced uneasily to where the tall, watchful figure of the scarred young man stood against the wall.

"A neat trick that, lowering your head I mean and muttering to yourself, but surely you know that it isn't necessary to vocalise your words when using a throat mike?" He nodded. "I see that you do and I imagine that the play-acting was for Wilson's benefit. It was wasted, Laurance. Wilson knows as much about the ultra beam as we do, the hypno-tuition is very effective and all the trained men have had a full course."

"I meant what I said," gritted the fat man doggedly. "You are clutching at straws, Hogarth."

"Not straws, Laurance. Never straws." Hogarth reached forward and pulled open the drawer at his side. Metal glinted from it, the smooth sheen of polished surfaces and the cold glitter of graduated dials. An ultra beam relay station.

"Listen," said the Admiral, and adjusted a control. Voices spilled into the silent room.

"Ship One calling Stellar. One calling Stellar. Answer please."

"Stellar here," snapped Hogarth, his words relayed from the microphone at his throat, "Hogarth speaking."

"Thank God!" Relief echoed in the thin voice.

"Trouble?"

"Not yet, but there's a ship following us, has been ever since we left Planet X."

"A Federation vessel?"

"I'm not sure. It appeared on the screens shortly after we left the rendezvous, seeming to come from the direction of Andromeda."

"From Outside?"

"Yes, sir."

"I see. Can you place the silhouette?"

"No, sir. It doesn't match any screen-pattern I'm familiar with, and none from the manual." Worry echoed from the thin voice. "I don't like it, sir. The thing isn't like any other ship I've ever seen, and I served through the last five years of the war."

"A moment." Hogarth stared at Laurance. "Are there any Federation ships of unusual design operating in the seventh decant towards Andromeda?"

"Not that I know of. Most of the Federation ships are busy re-establishing the trade and commerce routes within the known area. Why?"

"My ships came from Outside, about fifteen light years beyond the known area towards Andromeda. There is a planet there, a small place circling a dying sun. I cached my ships and materials there. If an unknown vessel has followed them..." He thoughtfully bit his lower lip.

"Ship One calling Stellar," echoed the concealed speaker. "Are you with me?"

"Yes."

"Ready to drop to planetary drive. Orders?"

"Normal landing."

"What about that ship following us?"

"Blast it," said Hogarth carelessly, and broke the connection. He looked at the fat man. "Well Laurance? Do you still want to arrest me?"

"Ships," said the Director heavily, and a chair creaked beneath his weight. "You wouldn't dare!"

"No?"

"You wouldn't! No man would!" He stared despairingly at the grim-faced Admiral. "You devil!"

"An elementary precaution, Laurance. An army must have ships and ships must have men. I had the ships, I salted them away a long time ago, together with a full stock of war material. But I needed men. Now?" He sucked in a deep breath. "Now I have both ships and men, and the galaxy is waiting."

He held out his hand.

"The gun, Wilson." He frowned as the tall young man hesitated. "Give me the gun! You need have no fear, your training is over, now we are ready to take what is ours and small things can be forgotten!" He nodded approvingly as Wilson broke the weapon and removed the charges. "Good. A wise precaution."

He stood, the empty gun poised in his hand, and smiled coldly at the huddled figure of the Director.

"Now what, Laurance? If you attempt to bomb Stellar my ships will devastate the habitable worlds. I have ten of them, Laurance, ten of the finest ships ever built. Warships, armed and armoured, and loyal men to run them." He glanced at the pistol in his hand. "You see? Even your guinea pig has failed you. My men know when they are well off, they know that I can lead them to victory, and knowing that, they will follow me to the death!"

He stood, his thin lips curved in a cold, proud smile, and around them, growing like the muted humming of a giant bee, swelling and roaring with the song of unleashed power, the heavy air trembled to the passage of mighty vessels of war as they dropped into planetary drive and swung into orbit around the planet.

The warships of the Stellar Legion!

CHAPTER 15

THE SHIP FROM OUTSIDE

Three times they circled the planet, their hulls glowing with the friction of their passage, through the thick air, and Laurance stood, like a thing of stone, counting them as they swept over the settlement.

"...seven. eight, nine... Nine! Nine ships!"

"Nine?" Hogarth frowned and turned to the ultra beam transmitter, its shrilling attention signal dying as he adjusted a control.

"Hogarth! Hogarth! Come in Hogarth!"

"Hogarth speaking. Come in."

"Ship One here. We're in trouble."

"Where is the other ship?"

"Blasted. I told you that we're in trouble. That vessel which was following us, the one I told you about..."

"The Federation ship?"

"Federation hell!" Brittle anger echoed in the voice vibrating from the speaker. "That's no Fed ship. It streaked down on us just as we dropped into planetary drive, must have been decelerating at fifteen gravities, and before we knew what happened it blasted ship Seven."

"Why didn't you attack it?"

"Attack it?" The voice snorted. "We wouldn't stand a chance. It got ship Seven amidships and the whole vessel went up in green flame. We can't fight weapons like that."

"Where is the ship now?"

"I don't know. It started to track us and we swung into orbit. Why do you think we're coming in so fast?"

"Why come in at all? Why don't you blast it in space?"

"Listen, Hogarth," snapped the voice, and it was tense with weariness and strain. "We're operating with skeleton crews and the automatics. How in the name of hell can we serve the guns, too? We want men, lots of them, and quick. I hope that your boys are ready."

"Are you insane?" Hogarth almost snarled into the microphone. "If you set down you won't have a chance, that ship, whatever it is, could pick you off one by one. Stay aloft and fight it, man. What chance could it have against nine of you? Ram it, sear it with your jets, set the fore torpedo tubes to automatic and fire tracking missiles. Damn it all! Do I have to tell you how to fight?"

"No, sir."

"Then keep off the ground. I…" He broke off as sound-thundered through the air.

Through the high windows, shaming the sun with its scintillating brightness, light streamed, a sharp, searing, blue-white radiance, and echoes rolled flatly over the desert mingling with the crystalline tinkling of shattered glass and the thin shouts of men startled into brief panic.

"That was ship Three," snapped the distant speaker. "That damned vessel, I…" The voice faded then suddenly filled the room with frantic warning. "Hogarth! The stranger is hovering over the settlement!"

"What!"

"Yeah. Looks as if they intend landing. They seem to be flashing a green ray of some kind, the same sort of thing they blasted the ships with. I…"

A peculiar humming filled the air, a strange, nerve-tearing vibration, and a brilliant shaft of green light swept across the desert, heading towards the clustered buildings of the settlement. Sand bubbled wherever the beam touched, bubbled and fused into a mass of dull glass, liquid and glowing heat.

Laurance stared at it, his fat body trembling as he tried to understand, then, as the beam swung towards them, a hand gripped his shoulder.

"Outside," snapped Hogarth. "Quick!" He almost thrust the Director through the narrow door.

A ship hovered over the settlement, a strange vessel, scintillating with pulsing waves of blue fire, ovoid and devoid of any trace of jets or other propulsion mechanisms. From a smoothly rounded portion of the hull the green ray emanated, tracing a smoulder-ing path over the low buildings, and men shrieked and dropped, screamed and ran from the beam of searing heat.

"Is that a Federation ship?" Hogarth squinted at it with nar-rowed eyes.

"No."

"Then it's an alien. It's from Outside!" The tall Admiral swore in savage bitterness. "Damn it, Laurance, I warned you that this would happen. He spun on his heel, his harsh voice rapping terse orders.

"Wilson! Rennie! Get the men out into the desert, scatter and deploy. Get weapons, all you can but get the Niones before any other. Attach formation. Move!" He grabbed Laurance and raced the fat man towards the open desert.

"What are you doing?" The Director flinched as the ray swept over a running group of men. "You'll never blast that down with Niones, it's too high."

"I know it." Hogarth dropped behind the shelter of a rock. Tear-ing at his tunic he ripped the concealed microphone from beneath his shirt and rapped terse orders. "Hello the fleet. Hogarth here. Ram that alien ship. Ram it."

"It'll land on the settlement if we do." The tiny voice reflected some of the distant speaker's sickness at the savage destruction.

"Never mind that. We'll take care of whatever's inside after they land, but you've got to bring down that ship. Hurry!"

He dropped the tiny instrument, and, grabbing the fat man, raced away from the path of the searing ray. Laurance grunted as he felt a wave of heat blister the skin on his back, then he was down again, rolling on the gritty soil, and staring up at Wilson and a dozen wild-eyed men.

"Stay down," snapped the young man. He saluted Hogarth. "Captain Rennie has deployed his men and the other Nione to the east. What orders, sir?"

"Wait until the enemy ship has landed. Hold your fire until the crew have emerged, I'll give the signal." Hogarth glanced at Laur-ance. "Better keep an eye on him, too, while you're at it. I'll go and check the rest of the defences." He wriggled away, a tall, lean, somehow ungainly figure, and yet Laurance was sorry to see him go. He stared at Wilson.

"What happens now?"

"For you, nothing. Just keep out of the way." He squinted at the swelling bulk of the alien ship. "We'll handle the rest, but I wish they'd hurry up and get that thing down."

Thunder rolled from the horizon. A swelling, snarling, blasting accumulation of sound, and a sleek vessel, its hull glowing red from friction, slammed down from out of the sun towards the alien ship.

Light blazed from the smooth ovoid of the strange hull. A series of pulsing gouts of green incandescence spraying towards the hurtling vessel, and, beneath the green fire, the stubborn metal of the nose of the warship glowed white hot and ran in molten ruin.

The ship struck!

Wilson cowered beneath the sudden blaze of blue-white radiance, shielding his eyes from the fierce glare, and felt his skin prickle to the thrust of gushing radiations. Noise rumbled through the air and fragments of debris fell around them, smoking scraps of metal and twisted sections of semi-molten hull. He blinked, staring towards the alien ship, his grey eyes widening with surprise.

It rested on the desert, its hull ripped and dented, the sand around it fused to a glassy mass. It heaved, stirring on the sand, and around it the pulsing blue glow of its strange drive flared and faded, flared again, then died away revealing a dully metallic, lead-coloured hull. From the rents in its hull things moved with a grim purpose.

Wilson swore, crouched down behind the slender barrel of the Nione, his fingers curved around the trigger and his grey eyes narrowed as he judged the distance between him and the aliens. Behind him a man retched in sudden revulsion and another, a new arrival to Stellar, babbled prayers to his forgotten saints. Laurance felt ill. He stared at the things advancing from the wreck of the alien vessel and fought an insane desire to get up and run, and run, and keep on running. He swallowed.

"What are they?"

"How should I know?" Wilson licked his lips. "Keep quiet now."

"Blast them," urged a man desperately. "Wipe them out before they get too close. Send them back into the hell they came from."

"Shut up!"

"But..."

"Shut up!"

The man fell silent and Wilson concentrated on the swift advance of the things from the wrecked vessel.

Tall they were, taller than a man, multi-tentacled and moving in a half-hop, half-crawl. Metal glinted from their appendages, and green fire spurted towards the deserted settlement, buildings collapsing in molten ruin.

"Heat rays," muttered Lauranee. "They've got heat rays."

From the other side of the settlement three shots echoed above the whining hiss of the alien rays.

Grimly Wilson stooped over his weapon.

Fire lanced towards the aliens, a searing beam of disrupted atoms, and, as they smashed a path through the heavy air, the sound of their passage thundered across the desert. A thing, half-seen and half-understood, flared and died, collapsing into a fine heap of grey ash. Another, another, then green fire spat towards them and the air was full of lung-baking heat.

Things fluffed and died in smouldering ash, spun and dropped as slugs ripped at their bodies, scattered and flung themselves towards shelter. Green fire sparkled and men shrieked as molten sand seared unprotected flesh, crisped arms and legs to charred ruin, and burned with all the fury of an opened hell. A man leapt to his feet, his eyes wide and his mouth spilling screams as he ran from the group to the safety of the desert. Wilson snarled, his hand dropping to his side, and lead whined from the pistol in his hand. The man staggered, fell, blood staining his tanned skin and his eyes glazing as he tried to force his dying body onwards.

Laurance felt sick.

"Did you have to do that?"

"Yes." Wilson ducked as a heat ray lashed towards him, dragging the Nione behind the shelter of a rock, and hugging the sand.

Again the Nione shouted its roaring challenge towards the aliens, joining the second energy weapon in rolling thunder, and traversing the exposed area in short, annihilating arcs. It jerked, grew hot and erratic, the swollen firing chamber almost radiating heat, but still Wilson served the weapon, aiming more carefully now, sharp-shooting, picking off the scattered aliens one by one. Finally he nodded to the waiting men.

"Right. On the double and shoot first. Attack!"

They surged to their feet, and, guns glinting in their hands, flung themselves forward across the fused desert. Others followed them, springing up from where they had lain hidden, waiting for the Nione guns to cut down the opposition, and the snarl of bullet weapons chattered from between the ruined buildings.

Wilson grunted and jerked his head at the fat man.

"Come on."

"Where to?"

"The ship." The young man gritted his teeth as he lifted the heavy bulk of the energy gun. "Hurry!"

Rennie met them halfway there.

The stocky captain was injured, one arm hanging limp and a charred hole revealing burned flesh. He had a man with him, a pale-faced lance corporal who nursed the squat bulk of a sub-gun, and he looked ill.

"Directing the mopping up," said Rennie. He glanced at the Nione. "I'm glad you brought that thing, my gun flashed-back on me," he looked at his arm, "and we may need more than bullet guns to clean this mess up."

Wilson nodded and advanced towards the waiting ship.

Two hundred yards from the hull he stopped, his grey eyes narrowed, and, with a sudden abruptness, set down the gun and swung the slender barrel towards a gaping rent in the dull grey metal.

"What…?"

Rennie fell silent as the young man gestured.

"I thought I saw something," said Wilson quietly. "A glint of metal. I…" The lance corporal screamed as green fire spat from the shadowy interior of the strange vessel.

Laurance caught the sub-gun as it fell from the lifeless hands, and its chatter joined the snaring thunder of the energy weapon. He knelt, aiming by instinct, and next to him the stocky captain blazed away with a pistol in his one good hand.

Before them things twitched and crawled as they spilled from the ripped hull. Metal gleamed among them and heat lashed at the three men, but the searing beam from the energy weapon made a scintillating barrier of stabbing destruction. Oddly shaped moving things advanced from the wreck, advanced and died in flaring gouts of energy, their grey ash coating the desert. They died, but in dying, they fought to the last.

Finally it was over, and Rennie stared dully towards the ruined hull and the thick pile of ash.

"They kept coming," he said dully. "Like ants walking into a fire, they just kept coming." He gulped and was suddenly very sick, more sick than he could have ever been over the destruction of human enemies. Laurance said nothing, and Wilson rose slowly to his feet, staring down at the fat man.

"Let's go," he said quietly. "There's nothing more we can do here now."

Silently the three men walked back to the shattered ruins of the settlement.

Hogarth was waiting for them when they returned. He sat on a chair in the shadow of a wall and listened to a stream of reports from hurrying men. He nodded towards them and gestured for them to sit.

"Good work, Wilson," he said. "You've earned a promotion for this. Those things in the ship could have wiped us out."

"An obvious precaution," said Wilson. He stared at his burned hands. "I don't think that they'll try it again, sir."

"No?" Hogarth shrugged. "Perhaps not, but where there is one ship there will be others."

"I didn't mean that, sir. I meant leaving their vessel to attack a colony. I don't think that what we killed in the ship were the same type of creatures as attacked us."

"I see. Are you certain of that?"

"No, sir." Wilson shrugged. Everything happened so fast, but I had the impression that they were slower moving, if you know what I mean. The ones that attacked us seemed far more ferocious and agile."

"You could be right, Wilson. I hadn't thought about it." Hogarth looked at the stocky captain. "How is your arm?"

"I'll live." Rennie shrugged. "What's the damage?"

"Surprisingly little. Three ships gone, two of them with crews, the one that rammed the alien was set on remote control. Most of the buildings wrecked and almost all the stores. Half of the new arrivals died in the initial attack, they are no loss, and we suffered fifty trained men and officers killed or wounded. It could have been a lot worse."

"Wilson killed a man," said Laurance suddenly. "Shot him down like a dog."

"Did he?" Hogarth stared at the young man. "Why?"

"He deserted his post, sir."

"And so you killed him. Good!" The tall Admiral stared at the fat Director. "You mustn't blame Wilson for doing what he had to do. We were in battle and one coward could start a panic. I would have done the same myself."

"But..." Laurance paused, then shrugged, knowing that, deep within himself, he agreed with the Admiral. War was war, and there was no place for the weak and timid when worlds were locked in combat. He became aware of Hogarth speaking.

"What?"

"I asked you what happens now, Laurance. Surely you know what this ship and the attack on us means?"

"Yes," said Laurance dully and tried not to feel panic.

He sighed.

"We shall have to rebuilt the Terran Fleet, of course, we dare not remain defenceless now that we know we are not alone in the galaxy." He stared at Hogarth. "Naturally, you will take full command."

"No." Hogarth smiled at the fat man's expression. "You can find some other to do that work. I will remain with my wolves, with the Legion I built from nothing. But you must continue to give me a free hand and to supply me with all I need." He shook his head as Laurance tried to speak. "I know what you're going to say, but

I too can learn a lesson. The Legion will be a volunteer force, you can offer any fit criminal the alternative say, of seven years with the Legion or serving his sentence in some prison or labour camp. They can have free choice, but, once they choose, there must be no whining. I have my own methods of training, and they are hard, but they produce men!"

"I agree," said the fat man drily. "They do produce a certain type of man, but how will you get enough to guard the Federation?"

"I won't, but that is your job, not mine." Hogarth leaned forward. "We can't protect the entire Federation. What we can do, and will do, is to raid enemy worlds. I shall set up a base on Planet X and from there we can scan the spacelanes for raiding vessels. We must explore, find out just what we are up against, and then, if they dare ever to attack our part of the galaxy, we'll blast them to dust!" He drew in his breath with a sharp hissing sound.

Laurance stared at him, half-afraid of the expression on his thin features, an expression reflected on the faces of both Rennie and Wilson. He nodded, feeling a strange sense of peace and safety.

"I agree. The Stellar Legion will be your responsibility and we depend on you to give us the time we need in order to rebuild the Terran Fleet."

"We will give you the time," said Hogarth quietly. "You can depend on it."

Laurance nodded, then, abruptly, put out his hand.

"It's a funny thing," he said as Hogarth stared at him. "A short while ago we were at each other's throats, and now, in the face of attack from alien worlds, we have forgotten those differences and are united in a common bond. Will you shake my hand?"

Hogarth nodded, and the two men stared for a moment into each other's eyes. Then the Admiral shrugged and his voice hardened.

"Now to work. I need fresh stores of food and equipment, uniforms and protective clothing against the heat ray, Nione guns, both heavy duty and hand weapons, medical stores..."

Wilson rose and walked away, the Admiral's voice fading into a muted drone behind him. It was a long way from being an orphaned waif, unnoticed, a thing of chance, a number in a forgotten record, to an officer in the Stellar Legion. A long way and the path had been hard, but now?

Sergeant Wilson drew a deep breath as he imagined the rosy future. Tomorrow he would be a lieutenant, the day after...?

He smiled as he strode across the sand.

He felt strangely proud.

Printed in Great Britain
by Amazon

15691253R00075